Essence Seekers is a fun and ingenious way to become acquainted with the world's spiritual marketplace. Urmila's storytelling is thought-provoking. Her cast of characters will take you through a cornucopia of genuine spiritual experience from a host of different disciplines. Explore and learn and spare yourself from the common pitfalls of a spiritual journey.

— Pranada Comtois
Author, *Wise-Love: Bhakti and the Search for the Soul of Consciousness*

Urmila Edith Best invites us on a brisk spiritual journey with Avid and his friends, an inner trek that brings us through a wide-spectrum doxography of the most enduring eastern "schools of thought." To comprehend these differing life-perspectives, Avid finds himself enrolling in actual school courses, in Acumen City's veritable university of spiritual paths and practices, each more bracing and vision-expanding than the last. All the while, Avid's persistent seeker's resolve empowers him to dodge all threats of diversion, ennui, and failure, with each step affirming in increasing clarity the truth of a higher reality opening within himself. As a trans-representation of India's classical sacred works of "connection" (yoga), Best deftly guides us into their rich and profound reaches coursing through the depths of human fulfillment, thoroughly beyond all self-imposed limits and limitations of conventional life.

— Krishna Kshetra Swami (Dr. Kenneth Valpey)
Oxford Centre for Hindu Studies

Essence Seekers is a very good allegorical tale, full of deep meaning and beautiful descriptive passages. I could relate to the many twists, temptations, and turns of Avid's journey. So many get lost, but he was able to remember and take full advantage of his teacher's instructions along the way. I enjoyed the read and found the characters intriguing and memorable.

— Alfred Ford
Philanthropist; Great-grandson of Henry Ford

In her groundbreaking new book, *Essence Seekers*, Urmila tells a profound and adventurous story of a quest for life's meaning, often engaging the classic technique of allegorical dialogue. Through a timeless narration, she directly speaks to our time, not an easy thing to do. This book will be a valuable companion to those who seek true wisdom in our troubled age.

— H D Goswami (Dr. Howard Resnick)
Visiting lecturer at GTU in Berkeley, University of Florida, Harvard, Yale, Cambridge, and Oxford; Author of *Quest for Justice* and *A Comprehensive Guide to Bhagavad-gita*

Told through the most brilliant allegories and enchantingly beautiful imagery, *Essence Seekers* is a masterful offering of simply delectable spiritual nectar and timeless wisdom. Anyone who is a genuine seeker of life's highest truths will find Best's account of an avid soul's journey towards deep meaning and authenticity to be personally relatable and eternally profound. As someone who is seeking to make a difference in the world in a spirit of servant leadership, I will certainly always treasure this book as a guiding compass towards my own spiritual enlightenment and that of those who I aspire to serve.

— Mpho MacChambers
Social activist and changemaker; Founder and executive director of Kula Education

Presenting spiritual journeys through fables is a respected tradition. However, far less traveled is the road of presenting through fables in English the many options for inner growth given in the ancient Vedic tradition. Urmila Edith Best guides us along this road expertly, making abstruse concepts accessible through an engaging narrative that reflects ordinary human struggles and extraordinary supra-human aspirations. By dextrously illustrating through incidents many of the metaphors given in time-honored spiritual texts, she brings their message to life, cautioning us about the many pitfalls on the spiritual path while also cushioning our journey through deepened self-understanding.

— Chaitanya Charan
Author of over twenty books on spiritual topics

Urmila's *Essence Seekers* is a masterful account of a journey—both inward and outward. We can identify with the characters and events, which foster in us detachment from the mundane and eagerness for the Divine. The book takes models from ancient sources and casts them in a contemporary—or timeless—setting. And it presents complex concepts in simple language and offers practical advice on how to negotiate the internal and external, and the apparently material and the spiritual, realms. It is said that when the beak of a parrot (suka) touches a ripe fruit, the fruit becomes even sweeter. In a similar way, Urmila had made the subject matter of this book extremely relishable. And her book may also inspire readers to delve into her sources—*Srimad-Bhagavatam* and *Sri Caitanya-caritamrta*—and thus enhance and accelerate their own journeys toward the Supreme.

—Giriraj Swami
Author of *Many Moons* and *Watering the Seed*

Such an enjoyable read, Urmila Edith Best's *Essence Seekers* took me on a delightful adventure into another time, another life—one filled with discovery and purpose. I expect this book will leave a lasting impact on any teenager or adult who embarks on a journey through its pages, and ponders the deep philosophical teachings creatively woven into the story.

—Kosa Ely
Author of *The Peaceable Forest*, *The Prince and the Polestar*, and *The Jaguar's Story*

Urmila Edith Best artfully weds timeless metaphors, allegories, and analogies to create the uniquely edifying fable, *Essence Seekers*. Be enriched and enlivened by this strangely familiar exploration of the world we inhabit, and discover how to progress spiritually despite this world's countless challenges.

—Visakha Dasi
Author, *Five Years, Eleven Months and a Lifetime of Unexpected Love*; Writer and co-director, *Hare Krishna! The Mantra, the Movement, and the Swami Who Started It All*

ESSENCE
SEEKERS

ESSENCE SEEKERS

A Quest Beyond the Forest of Enjoyment

Urmila Edith Best

Published by Padma Inc., 2018
Hillsborough, NC, USA

Quotes from God's Song are from Bhagavad-gita As It Is.
Quotes from the Bible are from various translations.
"The Tiger" poem is by William Blake.
The cow song is by Bhaktivinoda Thakura (1838-1914).

Printed by CreateSpace, An Amazon.com Company.
Available from Amazon.com and other retail outlets.

Illustrations by Phalguni Radhika Devi-dasi
and Padma-gopi Walsh.

Design by Michael Best.
Set in Horley Old Style, Brioso, and Cronos.

Version 1.3 (May 2018)

Dedicated to those who seek and
find the essence of life, and to my
teachers and guides on this journey.

Sweet and pleasing are literary ornaments like
metaphor. Without such poetic attributes there is
no communication of loving relationship (rasa).

(*Caitanya Caritamrita*, Antya 1.198)

Contents

About Journey Allegories

Each culture and tradition has inspirational stories, both historical and fictional, which describe how to find a successful and satisfying life. A persistent form of such stories is a journey allegory. In this genre, each character is an archetype. Names of the characters may be significant, and the protagonists in this tale — Avid (pronounced with the *a* like *apple*), Keen, and Sage — all have names indicative of their natures. (The other characters have names drawn from many languages to indicate their inclination, and these are listed at the end of the book as extra information for those who are interested.) In journey allegories, places, creatures, and human characters in the protagonist's external world are symbolic representations of internal changes in the protagonist. The literary device of travel is itself symbolic of the protagonist's inner progress. Typically, the plot in such allegories develops through a series of vignettes which make up the rising action, climax, falling action, and conclusion of the narrative. Some of the better-known examples of such allegories are Pilgrim's Progress (and its summary, Dangerous Journey), Hinds' Feet on High Places, Siddhartha, and The Alchemist. There are also inspirational allegories that, while not using the metaphor of a journey, move the plot mostly through a series of vignettes, some an essential part of the plot and some peripheral. Some examples are The Screwtape Letters and The Holy Man. Lesser known is Puranjana. The story in this book is a journey allegory, rooted mostly in Eastern traditions but also drawing from the West, that hopes to speak to the timeless and universal search for the essence of life within us all.

Where it Began

Really and truly this story was first told very long ago — well, one and a half billion people believe it really happened, so there's a reasonable chance it did. Before the Egyptians built the pyramids, and before the ancient Greeks or the Chinese had an advanced civilization — this story was told by a prodigy. Prodigies often become famous for clearly demonstrable skills — say, in music, dance, or mathematics. A prodigy in inner wisdom and insight may remain invisible to the world. It is said that there was a wise man who voluntarily had never said a word in his life. This was Jada. That name was not his given name. The meaning of Jada in the ancient tongue is *dull* and *foolish*. It was a name born of bullying and cruelty on the part of Jada's half-brothers and their friends, and it stuck as if his real name. By the time most children start to speak, Jada's understanding, insight, compassion, detachment, peace, and feeling of connection with all life had blossomed in ways rarely seen even in the great teachers and leaders in the world. He chose to become an absolute hermit to focus on inner meditation, but how was such a young hermit — merely a toddler — to join an order or retire to the caves of mountains? So, he became a hermit inside himself. He responded only enough to survive. His loving father tried until his death to educate his son, with no external success, though the boy learned all.

Of course, he did not appear particularly wise to anyone because he never spoke and barely appeared to hear or see. Nor did he make practically any effort to care for or maintain himself. After his father died when he was a teenager, he left his stepmother and half-brothers. He traveled and lived on whatever he could find or whatever he was given, without comment or complaint. Jada patiently bore even a murder attempt upon him, absorbed in his inner understanding. Perhaps, even though he was filled with compassion, he felt that the benefits of isolating himself from the world outweighed enlightening others. Many cloistered ascetics in numerous traditions have followed such lives. But, one day he broke his silence, and this story is the result.

Once, while Jada, strong in the prime of life, was walking along a main road, King R. Gana was traveling the same road in his palanquin. Near where Jada rested, the palanquin carriers also took a break. One of the four palanquin carriers suddenly complained of illness and left the king's service to seek treatment. King Gana then pressed Jada into slavery as the replacement carrier. The wise man carried the king's palanquin while trying to avoid stepping on insects and other creatures of the road, as was his habit. Needless to say, the king got a very shaky ride. The king then halted his carriers and came out of the palanquin to berate his newest palanquin carrier and to demand excellent service. No one knows why Jada decided at that point to speak for the first time in his life. But speak he did, and he told the king this story of merchants in a great forest. As soon as King Gana understood the story, he awakened to his inner nature and became a seeker of the essence of life. Jada's story was passed orally through many generations, and was put into writing a few thousand years ago, as is noted in the written account.

Much later, in recent times — more recent than the wise man and the king, at any rate — another part of this story was put in writing. It was around the time European colonists were first coming to the Western Hemisphere. A wealthy government officer in India under Islamic rule voluntarily decided to live in poverty in the Sacred Garden, becoming somewhat a recluse in the more traditional way. Those who recognized his wisdom and holiness called him a name that in the ancient tongue means *the servant who has mastered his mind and senses,* or a *servant leader* as we say in modern times. In a short form, he can be called Das G. His story starts where Jada's ends — with the determination to seek the essence of life — and tells of a journey through many obstacles, and with many helpers, to find that essence in a most personal way.

Here these two parts of the story find their rightful place together. But, the wise man who taught the king, and the government officer-turned-servant leader, never made it clear if the stories they told happened in a past distant to them, or within their own time, or would happen in the future. Perhaps these stories were not even from this planet. Therefore, we who hear this story today don't know if the vehicles used in the story have animals or motors running them, or if the messages sent back and forth are carried in someone's bags or via satellites. In this re-telling, readers may decide for themselves about such details. It could be — indeed it's very likely — that this story happened long ago, is happening now, and will take place in some future time as well. Of course, the names and details would be different each time, but yet the most important parts of the story would still be the same.

So, we begin…

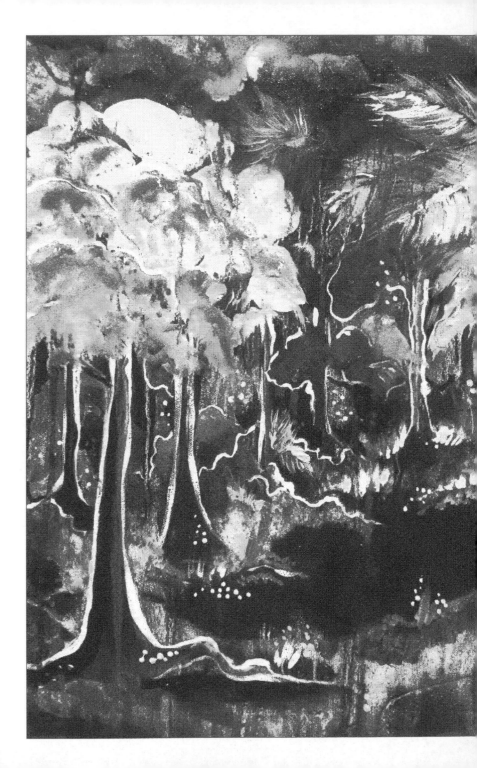

PART ONE

Forests

The Merchants

Once upon a time, a group of many families traveled together collecting various items in the forest, hoping to sell those items in villages and cities and become wealthy. Avid's family had spent so much time in the forest, it seemed to him that they lived there. Now nearly twelve years old, his earliest memory in the forest was of when he was maybe three or so. He had done something naughty — he forgot quite what it was — when Grandma told him that the wisest people learn by listening and watching, and not by doing foolish things. Since then he tried to carefully pay attention to those around him and to the natural world. As part of a large nomadic group and the youngest of five children — two older brothers and two older sisters — he had plenty of people to watch. And the forest provided much from which to learn, as well. Today he was observing insects on the forest floor.

Avid's mother, Duma, checked that the flower she had put in her hair earlier was still fresh. *Wish it were jewels instead of a flower.* The darkening sky signaled time to put up tents and build a fire. Duma sighed and turned to her husband, Tavis. "Not much we can profit from today, my dear."

Tavis shrugged and started to pound tent pegs into the ground. He was almost as well-built as his two oldest sons, and his pounding seemed effortless both because of the habit of the task and his strength. Birds called and seemed to laugh as they went into the trees for the night. As colored objects turned to silhouettes, bats replaced birds as lords of the sky. A slight chill rode on the breeze. As soon as the tent was up, Duma and Tavis found themselves calling in unison, "Mohah, Bron, Sarala, Pena, Avid!" and they smiled into each other's eyes at the mixture of their voices. As the five also answered in unison, "We are ready!" the couple's smiles widened into grins.

"Good children, those," Tavis said to no one in particular, though Pena, the closest in age to Avid at fifteen, heard her father and felt a quiet warmth fill her as she brought in the dried fruits which had been slowly dehydrating over a low fire. She seemed unaware of her natural beauty as she focused on her work. Mohah, Avid's oldest sibling at nineteen, was well-skilled in managing the day's jobs. He pushed a stray curling hair out of his eyes and with his muscular arms, covered a wagonload of wood with rain protection. It was a lot of wood, but just a common variety, useful for fuel and for furniture for the poor. Bron, at age eighteen the second son, brought in herbs for sorting and drying. These were mostly common mints. Some of the more valuable seeds he picked were also in his box, though there were not many of them. He handled the herbs and seeds with the kind of care one would give to precious and rare jewels, looking everything over carefully to select only the best. Though as strong as his older brother, Mohah, there was a grace in his slender fingers that one might expect to find in a fine craftsman or a surgeon.

As usual, even though Avid said he was ready, he continued to play with Keen, his best friend for many years. Duma watched them for a few minutes before calling him again. She saw that the boys seemed to be examining forest creatures, capturing some, looking at them, and then letting them go. And Avid was singing to the creatures. *We named him Avid, and later we learned that his name means one who is inclined to be eager and enthused. Ah, when we heard that, we hoped he would be ambitious.* She sighed and put her hands on her hips. *That boy needs to be more practical. And have more practical friends.* "Keen, will you eat with us or your family tonight? Avid! You said you were ready and then you went back to your play."

"I think our family is eating with yours," Keen answered and went over to the cooking fires where his father was already eating.

Avid came over to his mother and peered into the wooden box she was working over. "Grandma says…"

Duma briefly looked at her mother-in-law and sighed. "Are you going to tell me tall tales from Grandma again?" Duma then said into the box.

"But, Momma!" Avid sat on the ground.

"Get off that wet ground. You'll get dirtier than I can clean when we're out here in the forest."

"Grandma says we're lost," Avid said quickly enough that his mother couldn't interrupt.

"Depends what you mean by *lost*," Sarala cut in as she came over while Avid stood up and their mother brushed off the seat of his pants. Sarala, at sixteen their third child and Avid's oldest sister, rolled her eyes at her little brother's inquisitiveness and then turned to their mother. "Dinner's ready and Grandma helped me tonight, Momma, along with some of the cousins. We had enough to invite another family. Maybe Grandma invited two families."

"It may be a lot, but simple fare is still simple fare," Duma replied, still looking into the box and sorting stones. Sarala looked away, and then went back over to the fires quickly as her family members, Keen's family, and another family brought plates, helped themselves, and sat on rocks and logs to eat.

The firelight highlighted a bit of color in the circle of people who were surrounded by ever-encroaching darkness. There was hushed talk as they ate, with some alternating laughter and crying from the little ones. "Are we really lost, Grandma?" Avid asked while sitting down next to her.

"I'm sure of it, my boy," she said, putting down her bowl and staring at the rising moon. "The forest has been getting more and more dense. I'm sure we'll find villages where we can sell what we're collecting, but we've completely lost the way to get home.

We started into the forest to get items for a little trouble, bring them back to our homes in the village, and sell at a profit. But…"

"We had to go too far, right?"

"Yes, I'm afraid so. We couldn't find much close to home, and we've gone so far that the paths back cannot be found. Your parents and others don't want to tell you, but it's the truth. We'll have to settle in another village in a foreign land, or stay nomads."

"What's a nomad?"

"Someone whose home moves with them, and who has no real shelter other than a tent, dear boy."

Duma came from behind and put her hand on her mother-in-law's shoulder, "Why are you scaring the boy, Ma?"

"Oh, Duma, we've been in foreign lands so long; there's no use hiding the fact anymore. And that boy is always eager to know. He talks in more grown-up ways than lots of the grown-ups."

When Avid finished his meal, he noticed that his oldest brother, Mohah, was washing the plates and pots. "Doesn't Momma do that?"

"When you have more, share it," Mohah responded, "and tonight I have more energy than she does." He patted his youngest brother on the head and playfully punched his arm.

Avid gave his bowl to Mohah for washing, and moved from the fire. He watched the bats as the sky filled with stars. "Where is home, really?" he whispered to the night until his nodding head and closing eyes allowed no further reveries.

The Honeybee

The next morning Duma told the children that the entire group would camp for a few days in the spot they had found, because of proximity to water, food, and forest resources. After breakfast, everyone twelve and older went foraging. Grandma was watching about twenty of the younger ones, and Avid wandered a bit out of her vision. He was old enough that she didn't worry much about him anyway, he had noticed.

As Avid wandered, he dropped a trail of bright red seeds, a kind that taste terrible to birds and take long to sprout. "Path marker seeds," Sarala called them. He also marked trees with a soft red rock whenever he made a turn. Various insects shuffled or darted away from his careful feet, but he wasn't in any hurry even if some beetles were. As the forest warmed, Avid sat on a rock partially in the sun, moving as little as possible. Soon, birds landed on branches near him, probably unaware of his presence. *Where is home? Where is home? It has been so long since we were in any place we could call home. Momma and Dad and everyone keep collecting things, promising we'll go home, sell, and be rich, but we are just wandering, collecting, and selling in towns along the way, without ever going back. And we're on the way to where? No one seems to know, and no one wants to answer me.* Avid shifted his weight slightly to the other foot but no birds flew, and ants continued to walk over his shoes.

Thirst finally drove Avid from the rock. Moving slowly as he walked further, he scanned the area for any and all signs of life. A squirrel ran up a tree, and dragonflies mated in the air. Finally, after many twists and turns, all carefully marked, he heard water.

I wonder if this is the river Sarala's been going to, for cooking water? Avid had to make a few more turns before he got there. "Oh," he said aloud, causing some birds to fly, "this isn't the river, but a smaller stream! I wonder if anyone in our group has been to this part of the forest!"

He unhooked his water bag and opened it, carefully putting the lid on a grassy patch so as not to get dirt in it. Dipping the bag into the stream, the water quickly gurgled into it, but didn't fill it, as the water was too shallow by the bank. Removing his footwear, Avid carried the bag out a bit, dumped out what was already there, filled it again from the clearer, fast-running flow, swished the water around, dumped it again, and then allowed it to completely fill. Then, still standing in the stream, he took a long drink, dumped the rest, cleaned it yet again, and re-filled. The sun, still early in the sky — Grandma would be worried if he was gone too long — gently touched the moving water, creating diamonds of dancing light. The water was just cold enough to be refreshing but not painful on his calves and feet as he carefully walked back to the shore.

A ray of sunlight hit the area near where the lid lay on the grass. *Why didn't I see these before?* Dozens — or hundreds — of flowers grew there. Tiny flowers seemed to be looking expectantly at the sun, and even smiling. Some large honeybees hovered around the flowers. Avid's picking up the lid and putting it on the water bag didn't seem to faze the bees at all. Then, somehow, all the forest sounds stopped. The water, the wind, the bees, the birds, rustling leaves — all became suddenly and inexplicably silent. *This is very strange.* Inquisitiveness filled Avid as he found himself stunned. Not frozen, exactly, as he felt he could move if he so willed it, but rather it seemed as if he was aware that he had no desire for movement. *Only to be, not to do. Yes, only to be.* In the silence and stillness — for everything around him seemed to have stopped moving — there came a different awareness. *My mind is still and I am just watching my calm mind,* he thought in wonder and curiosity.

Then, while the stillness and silence remained, one creature

started to move. It was a large honeybee, with copious pollen on its legs and a belly swollen with nectar. The bee began to glow, and no longer looked like a bee at all, but like some sort of otherworldly or celestial being. A sense of quiet awe filled Avid, as if the glow of the bee—who seemed no longer to be a bee at all—was also inside of him, or produced by him. *I can feel myself glowing as if light fills me and comes from me. But it's a soft light, like when Sarala hugs me or when I eat something I like. And, what is that bee? Is it a bee at all? Are the bee and I glowing together, or do we each have our own light? Where is the light everywhere coming from?* These were gentle questions floating in his mind, questions that were disinterested musing rather than insistent urges to know.

The being that was no longer really a honeybee looked deeply at Avid, though the light around it made Avid feel, rather than see, its eyes. And he felt, and knew, its words, rather than heard them, yet the words were clear. "Avid, your real home is not of this world. Only the nectar seekers find it. That nectar is the essence of life. Those who seek nectar in this forest find it, but those who seek profits from selling the goods of the forest travel a path where no nectar seekers can be found."

As stillness and silence had heralded the divine being, now sounds again filled the forest as birds called, branches moved, and water ran over rocks. The being had simply vanished. Somehow the forest felt more alive than before, more full of mystery, yet it was also unchanged. *Was that real? The glow is still within me, but just a bit. It seems more real than what is now, what is normal.* Avid started walking, retracing the trail back to the encampment almost automatically. *Oh, I'm walking back to camp already, but I wanted to explore more.* He stopped for a moment, and looked around at other paths to try. Warmth filled him and light streamed brightly through the leaf canopy. *Did I say "already?" It's late! The sun is at mid-morning! I must have been a long time with the bee, or whatever it was.* Avid started to go faster, uncaring if his louder footsteps startled birds, bugs, and various creatures, though he was careful not to step on any of them.

Various Bodies
and Clay Figures

Grandma was busy washing a little child, with her back to Avid as he returned to camp. Avid went over to a group of other kids around his age, who were busy exploring ant trails. For a while he looked over at Grandma every few minutes until he caught her eye and she smiled. *Good! I wasn't missed! I wonder if that's because she didn't know I was gone, or because she trusts that I can explore a bit?*

"Hey, Avid!" Keen poked Avid and the two started to tussle. Soon, a number of boys were wrestling and stirring up the dirt. Gradually they started looking at the ants again.

"Keen, how many different types of bugs are there, anyway?"

"Ah, the minibeasts! Hey, let me show you something." Keen motioned Avid into a large tent, circular and domed. Keen's family had been able to sell some valuable wood in the last village and had purchased a new tent. "Amazing tent, huh?" Keen's smile was tight, but his eyes glittered as he scanned around. "My older brother doesn't get to stay here, you know. He's too old, and has his own place. But his place is not so nice. You want to look around here?"

"What about the minibeasts?"

"Oh, right."

In a corner of the palatial tent were several boxes. At least they looked like boxes from a distance. As the boys drew closer, Keen explained their contents. Avid saw so many varieties of insects, each frozen in a tiny replica of their own habitat. "Dead ones?" Avid didn't want to look squeamish, but he still felt the glow from his meeting with the bee and wasn't in the mood for death.

"I take that as quite a compliment," Keen straightened up and took a deep breath. "I made these out of clay mixed with colors from rocks. And I study how they live. Here, in this box," he said to the tent wall as he tugged on a large container, "are my models of every creature in the forest we've seen. Plants, too."

"The last time I looked at your clay figures they were just — well, simple things."

Keen nodded. "I decided not to show anyone until I learned how to make them really well. Even you."

Avid carefully looked at each creature, each plant. He wanted to spend hours here, and indeed, he did, over the next few days. On the third day, Keen left Avid alone with the exhibits. While looking at the clay bees, Avid thought of his strange encounter. He hadn't told anyone, not even Grandma. *Nectar seekers — I wonder what that means*, he mulled as he examined the detail of the clay bee's environment.

For a long time — or so it seemed — Avid forgot himself and felt that he was becoming each of the creatures he examined. *A tree yearns for the sun upwards and water downwards. It aches and stretches, gropes and touches. It seeks the riches of the forest as we do, but doesn't sell them. Ah, the trees sometimes give their riches away as fruits or flowers, or lose those riches to thieves, such as when we wound the trees to get sap, resin, or wood.*

Keen returned and noticed Avid's expression of absorption. "Can you feel the trees, Avid?"

Avid looked at Keen and slightly nodded, wordlessly.

Keen continued, "Remember my uncle who lives in the village we passed last full moon? He tells me that we have many lives, and we have lived in all these bodies. Each creature in this forest is trying to get wealth just as we are. Ha! But we are far cleverer. They collect the wealth, and we take it from them."

That night, Avid had a strange dream. The honeybee took the

form of a glowing celestial being, or maybe a saint or teacher, or maybe both. "Look!" the being said. "Look, feel, and remember!"

"Then, in the dream," as Avid told Keen in the morning, "I looked at my hands and they were wings. I flew and buzzed in the air. My thoughts and feelings were only hunger and food. Quickly, everything changed and my hands were stiff like wood, able to stretch and grow but not flex. I stretched towards light going up, and water going down, just like I felt when looking at your tree models. And I felt fear of the axe, fear of the wounds to get my resin and sap, fear of the birds and insects who drill in me, fear of the fires from which I couldn't run. Again, in an instant, when I looked at my hands they were like fins and my breath was strange, taking water in and out. I was in soft darkness with only filtered light, and underwater. Whether asleep or awake, my eyes were open and I continued to move, feeling only hunger and fear, but no thirst. So strange to have no thirst! In an instant, my arms turned to wings of many colors, and I could soar so high, catching the warm updrafts. Hunger again drove me and my food was small creatures. In that form, I felt thirst and feared only humans.

"I went through so many bodies in the same way—a deer, lion, and everything between. In each form I felt great fear, hunger, and (except when I was a fish), thirst. What was most strange, Keen, was that I also was in many human bodies, where I felt not only desires for food and safety, but also the same questions I feel now. And, even stranger was that in my dream I was also in bodies that were made of light—with great power and knowledge."

"Was there fear in those bodies too, Avid?" Keen asked. They were sitting behind the tents, almost whispering.

"Yes, but not so much. I felt answers to my questions, a little bit, but not complete. But there was a kind of freedom and joy in the light bodies that wasn't there in the bodies I had like those here. But that's not all. The honeybee creature told me that in all those bodies, even the light forms, I was no better than I am now, son of merchants in a forest, looking to make a profit, far from home. Strange dream, Keen!"

"Yeah, for sure."

Avid looked at his friend and then picked at his fingernails as if something was stuck there. *I told him only about seeing the strange bee creature in a dream, but I didn't tell him I actually met such a being. Maybe I should tell him that, too...but if the dream is weird, how much weirder is what really happened?* "Uh, Keen—"

"Avid! Where are you?" Grandma called. "Come help me with this wood!"

Avid didn't want to wait for Grandma to rebuke him for not being "practical" enough, and ran to help. He gradually discovered that the longer a secret is kept, the harder it is to set free.

Tigers and Jackals

"Nothing more in this place," Duma said in the evening as they sat around the fire, drinking soup.

Almost in unison, Mohah and Bron said, "Selling time tomorrow!"

That evening, most of the group gathered to give thanks to the lords of the forests, the rivers, the mountains, and the sky. Keen's father lead the ritual to ask the one Lord of All for protection from injury, disease, poverty, and enemies.

The next day everyone loaded vehicles with everything they had collected, along with tents, cooking materials, and whatever personal items each had. They slowly drove away from camp, away from previous villages, away from the depths of the forest, seeking a road in a new direction. No one really knew what the next destination would be, but a road is bound to lead to human habitation—buyers for their goods.

On the way they stopped to eat. Bron helped his younger sister, Sarala, set up a fire so she could prepare a quick meal. Most of the members of the group stretched their legs and walked around. Avid decided to try again. He easily found Keen as the tent they carried on their vehicle was so large and colorful. "Hey, you know that strange being like a bee in my dream I told you about?"

"Yeah," Keen said as he watched his older brother who was at a distance. "Hey, I got to help my brother with his stuff. He's got a lot of stuff and it's not balanced." Keen started to walk away, and then broke into a run.

Avid sang quietly as he walked slowly back to where Sarala was starting to serve lunch. *Maybe some things should stay unsaid. Even to good friends. For now.* He took a plate and ate slowly. *Yeah, I do want to be a nectar seeker.*

Before arriving at a road, night began to dominate the sky, and the group decided to camp in an open grassland, like a savanna. It was too dry in this area for the forest to intrude, as a mountain range blocked the rain. The open feature of the area made it easier to see what lurked about. Jackals started howling nearby. Tavis, Mohah, and Bron reached for various weapons to keep near them as they settled down after the evening meal. After a few minutes, Grandma tapped her son quietly on the shoulder. "Tavis, come quickly and quietly to see this. A tiger is near."

In the bushes near their encampment was, indeed, a tiger relishing the flesh of a large deer. Tavis and his mother had the finely-honed forest craft to observe her while being unobserved themselves. As they watched, the satiated tiger very slowly walked away and slept. They glanced briefly at each other, their thoughts instantly known to each other without words—*Should we kill the tiger for its skin?* Doubt and greed contested in him, and just as Tavis was about to try for a kill, a lone golden jackal crept out of the bush. Looking from side to side, the jackal spotted the sleeping tiger. Tavis lowered his weapon, deciding that watching was the only reasonable policy. Quietly, the jackal uncovered the deer carcass and ate to his satisfaction. As darkness increased, Tavis and his mother returned silently to the camp, leaving the thieving jackal and sleeping tiger in peace.

After finding a road, the group a few days later made it to a village. The group's camping routine changed as many families found accommodations in the homes of villagers. Villagers came to view the goods before market day, a good thing for sales. Everyone talked among themselves about the goods and their desires grew.

Pena and Sarala walked with their mother into a friendly villager's home to arrange dinner, glad to be cooking in a regular kitchen instead of an open fire. Mohah, Bron, and Avid moved and sorted their goods for market day. And Tavis secured everything.

Market day was chilly, clear, and with a brightness that fooled one into thinking the weather would be warmer than it was. The travelers were setting up their wood, medicinal and cooking herbs, dried fruits, useful stones, minerals, and some animal skins. *I hope they got the skins only from already dead animals,* Avid thought as he saw the furs lining one table. Suddenly there were loud voices from Keen's family. Keen's older brother, a grown man ready for his own family, nearly wept as his father accused him again and again of taking their rare woods. The other families kept their distance, leaving Keen's family to settle the dispute themselves. After some hours, while others set up tables and sold goods, Keen's brother left in disgrace. No one knew where he went.

"Jackals steal the tiger's meat," Tavis remarked to his mother.

"Some tigers steal from other tigers," Grandma replied, looking at Avid rather than Tavis.

Avid thought about whether or not to talk to his friend, Keen. *Better to offer sympathy now, or wait until things aren't so raw?* In the end, he decided to go to the house where Keen's family was staying as if nothing had happened.

"Avid!" Keen quickly pulled him back out the door and to the yard behind the house. "Best not to come inside right now. I was hiding, working on my clay."

"Oh, what creatures were you making?"

Keen looked around and didn't say anything for a while. "You know, Avid, about tigers and golden jackals?"

Avid was silent. *He must be really upset. Of course, all us forest merchants know such things.* After quite a pause, Avid simply nodded.

"Well, I was in the middle of sculpting a golden jackal eating a tiger's meal, and the tiger allowing it. Then my brother got accused of stealing. I mean, within a family, how can it really be stealing?" Keen picked up some dirt, wet from the previous night's rain, and started to knead it into a shape like a tiger head.

"You two were never very close."

"No, but a brother is a brother. I should go back inside. Come by tomorrow, ok?"

Avid's family did well, selling nearly everything, but another family had made a huge profit. That family was unusual in that only the father collected goods from the forest, while the mother and children were, as Duma sometimes said, "As idle and playful as tiny tiger cubs." Yet, after their large sale, the mother went to the local village shops and emerged looking like a fancy city lady. The children carried big bags of playthings newly purchased.

"Will be a heavy cart, but it will be full of nothing to sell," remarked Mohah to Avid, when Avid's curious eyes danced on the bags of toys those children carried. "Just a burden."

Tavis and his mother exchanged glances. "There are many ways for jackals to steal from tigers," Grandma said with a wink.

"Some tigers let golden jackals steal from them, Grandma," said Mohah. "A family partnership of jackal and tiger, thieves in the name of family!" And they all laughed as they went to a satisfying dinner.

Gadflies, Mosquitoes, Locusts, Birds of Prey, and Rats

It was great to be in a village and a real bed. Grandma had made friends with the elder members of the host family, and Sarala was trying out a new recipe with the vegetables they bought from the sale of their goods. Duma finally said good night to her hosts and entered a night of torture from gadflies and mosquitoes. Seems there was swampland near the village, and this time of year with mostly cool nights and warm days was perfect for the pests. Duma had always found that such insects bothered her much more than they did others. Something in her blood and sweat, the healers had said and shrugged. Oh, to hear the insects buzzing but not be able to find them! All night she tossed and turned, waking and then dozing, filled with anxiety about sleeping. Slap! Duma hit her own face and neck, trying to kill the insects, to no avail. Slap!

At breakfast, Duma dragged herself to the table, with bleary eyes and a blank expression. Grandma looked at her for some time. "Trouble is around us," Grandma said.

"Trouble is everyone's life companion," Mohah said, as if repeating an oft-heard truism.

Avid looked up from his bowl of fruit, specialty items bought from the sale of some of the rocks and minerals. "What trouble, Grandma?"

Bron and Tavis seemed to Avid to eat especially fast, never raising their eyes from their food. "Someone is saying that someone said we stole from Keen's family, that his older brother was either innocent or had help. They're looking at how much money we made from the sale," Grandma replied.

"Who?" asked Duma.

"Can't tell, Momma," interjected Mohah. "They're all around us. We hear the rumors and accusations, but we can't tell who is spreading them."

Grandma put down her bowl. "We don't even know what they are saying. People come up to me and say things such as, 'I'm so sorry folks are accusing you. I believe you, don't worry,' and I am not sure what they are talking about. If I ask they don't say."

"Can we do anything, Grandma?" Avid asked. Tavis and Mohah got up to wash, and Sarala and Pena grabbed each other's hands. Their hosts had finished breakfast earlier, and weren't around, but now Avid felt like perhaps they were really in the other room, listening, maybe even plotting.

"Not really, Avid," Grandma sighed.

"See, Avid," said Mohah, "if we don't say or do anything, people will assume we are guilty, and if we defend ourselves people will think we are guilty. We're not even sure what they are saying; we're taking a good guess."

"Makes it hard to sleep," said Duma. "Don't know what's worse—the gadflies and mosquitoes, or the whispers of envious, critical people."

Indeed, throughout the next night Duma and Tavis each only slept in short, five-minute intervals. Their minds constantly scanned their lives, trying to find who could be saying what terrible thing about them. Even if they could quiet their minds for a moment, then the gadflies and mosquitoes woke them.

Avid, however, had a different night. For the first hour, thoughts of unseen critical people raced through his mind. *What will happen to our family? What about my friendship with Keen? Will we stop traveling with the group? Will there be a trial? Is someone in our family actually guilty?* Fear, grief, and anger took turns coursing through Avid's body, releasing chemicals that grabbed his mind and shook it from side to side. Then, gradually, he remembered the bee, and the shining form it had taken. *"Do not seek profit in this world if you want to find your home." Yes, the bee said something like that. Can't profit also mean others thinking well of us? Profit for… what does Grandma call it? My ego, yes. Wanting others to think well of me is like wanting to make a profit for my ego!* A peace then filled Avid, a peace he could hardly describe, like the stillness of the forest when the bee was speaking. It was a peace he would need in the days ahead, though in that moment, the peace simply allowed him to fall deeply into untroubled sleep.

Keen and Avid continued to meet most days, and Keen assured him that no one in his family heard any rumors about Avid's family helping Keen's brother. Avid's peace was such that he was not in need of relief, yet felt grateful for his friend's concern. Some of the other boys shunned Avid, even when Keen defended him.

The group stayed in the village for some time, but Duma hardly slept at night, although the bed was comfortable. She kept hearing from friends about how others were criticizing her family but, without being able to find either who or why, her mind and heart filled with unremitting anxiety. She felt as if the mosquitoes of critics in the day and the insect mosquitoes at night conspired to give her no peace. Gradually she grew so irritable and ill from lack of sleep that she was pale and thin. Tavis worried about his wife on top of his worry about the critics, and it was nearly too much to bear.

Duma became so exhausted that she found it difficult to do anything she normally did. It seemed her body was a great weight she was dragging around, and her mind seemed full of fog. After nearly two weeks with hardly any sleep, she dragged herself on a sunny mid-afternoon to a shady orchard and sat beneath the trees. She had been born into a happy family, or at least a family that appeared to be happy. Her father was an expert craftsman, mostly working with metals, and her mother ran the business part of her husband's crafts. As she leaned against the tree, without energy to direct her thoughts or feelings, she found her mind drifting to her childhood. Closing her eyes, Duma felt herself again a young girl. *Ah, that day! That was the day! I looked out the window and saw that proud girl! Proud....* Duma's closed eyes swelled with tears, which dripped slowly down her cheeks. *Was that girl really proud? Yes, of course. There was no other reason she said so many terrible things about me, and my sister, and... even my mother. Terrible things. She wore such beautiful clothes. If I could get money like she had, then people would want to please me, and I would be happy.* Duma opened her eyes and wiped the tears. She whispered to the tree as she touched its rough bark, "Your fruits are almost ready and will be worth a lot in harvest time. Someday I will be rich, dear tree, as rich in wealth as you will be in fruit." Duma smiled a little and lifted her head. *That proud girl's parents ran the town, but I will run more than a town. But, right now, I wish I could sleep.* Duma lay down on the ground and immediately fell asleep. A few moments later the gadflies found her and buzzed in her ears. Mosquitoes bit all the exposed skin, and some bit through her clothes. "Away! Away!" she yelled, suddenly awake. After leaning against the tree again for a while in resignation, Duma finally got up and dragged her tired body back to the house they were staying in. Somehow, she was able to avoid Tavis or any of the children seeing her return, so she wouldn't have to explain her still swollen eyes.

Many large fertile fields surrounded the village where they stayed, and a good number of the villagers engaged in agriculture. Some only grew a few vegetables and fruits for their family, but many had large areas covered with grain. The time when the group stayed in that particular village just happened to be key to the harvest — a time when the seeds of the grains that grew overwinter had just been planted, and when the summer and autumn harvest was nearly ready. It was a dangerous time because in these few weeks every year the crops were the most vulnerable to pests. And that year the pests were bad.

While Tavis and his family — except Avid, whose peace continued to flow in him — worried about their traveling group's acceptance of them, their host family fell into deep despair and grief. The locusts had come! The dreaded locusts came rarely, and years would go by without seeing one. But this year swarms covered the fields and ate much of the crop that would have been harvested in a few days. What the locusts did not eat, rats consumed. There was always some damage from rats each year. But when the locusts and rats combined, the cost was immense. If that wasn't bad enough, the crow population seemed to have expanded, and the crows were eating the precious seeds that the families counted on to produce food in the spring. Villagers put up scarecrows, and even paid young boys to stand in the fields at various times of the day, to run after the birds. The village wouldn't starve, as they had an emergency supply of food, but times would be hard for many months. Sadness, grief, and fear covered the village like a thick blanket of fog on a chilly day.

Mohah and Bron sat quietly by the stream that ran through the village, its main water supply. Mostly, they both looked straight ahead at the water, sometimes throwing in a small stone. "Human thieves, insect thieves, mammal thieves, bird thieves," Bron said to the ground after some time.

There were many minutes of only the sounds of the water and wind. "We work so hard and others take it," Mohah almost spat as he spoke.

Finally, Bron looked right at his brother, his face slightly flushed and nostrils flared. "This is all we've got, you know? Just this life, this world, this place, our food, our things, our money, our family, our group! That's it! It's here and now and our home! And it's so…so…" He looked at the stream again, throwing in a large rock this time that sent powerful ripples and scared a frog.

"So nasty?" Mohah made a sound that was not exactly a laugh

or a grunt. "So nasty. All we have, and always in danger. Shaky. Ugh. Hey, let's get back for the meal. I would like to stay in this village for a while in order to take a bit of vacation from hard work, and then, I hope when we leave we go home."

"Home," said Bron flatly as they both rose. "I hardly remember what that is anymore."

Hunger and Thirst

The host villagers said they were happy to keep Tavis and his family as guests, yet it was clear that the attacks on the fields by locusts, crows, and rats had put them in difficulty. Smiles were scarce, and sharing food was without enthusiasm.

"Time to move on," Tavis said simply, one evening after the meal.

"Is the rest of the group ready to travel again?" asked Mohah. "I know I'm not. We worked hard for so long in the forest, and I want some rest."

"There's no rest here with the mosquitoes and the critics, anyway," Duma grumbled. "I'm ready to go."

"Time to move on," Tavis repeated. Sarala thought of cooking again outside, Pena of how hard it would be to find fruits in the growing chill, Bron of how he'd like to set up a shop selling herbal medicines but let someone else find the herbs in the forest, and Mohah just felt a firm decision that went to his core, a decision to accept his life as one of difficulty and hard work for the family. Grandma hoped she continued to have the strength and energy to mind the young ones.

Avid was, perhaps, the only one in the family to feel some anticipation. *Maybe I will find the path of the nectar seekers and learn about our real home beyond all this. Maybe I will see the bee again. Is that peace I've been feeling the same thing as the nectar the bee told me about? I want to be a real nectar seeker.* Singing softly, slightly smiling, Avid went to pack his things and help the family move everything to the cart.

There followed another night in the village for Duma of mosquitoes and sleep broken by anxieties about critics. Early the next day they started to arrange to leave. "Where are your walking shoes?" Duma screamed at Pena for perhaps the tenth time that day. Then she turned to her husband, "Tavis! Is the rest of the group going? Will we be alone in the forest? What madness are you taking us into?"

She's so tired, Avid looked away to escape being the next object of her wrath.

"Duma, just let's go. I've talked to the others. Whoever is coming is coming," Tavis said to the boxes and bags he lashed onto the cart.

"Maybe you are actually a thief, and that's why we're going now! Is that it? Are you hoping that by running away we will escape the accusations?" Duma almost screamed.

Grandma rounded up everyone except Duma, even Mohah, "I need your help over here," she said softly to them.

"Where are you taking all my helpers, Mother?" said Duma with an edge to her voice, a little too loudly. "Do you want to leave me to do everything alone?"

"We'll help you directly in a bit," replied Grandma, looking square at Bron, who was ready to yell back at his mother. "Right now the best help we can give you is over in the house."

"You and your mother are a great team!" Duma yelled at Tavis as he arranged things in the cart. "How will we survive in the forest without the whole group? Who is coming? Why won't you answer me?" After some time, Duma collapsed next to the cart and sobbed.

Tavis ignored her and continued packing. Perhaps he could have comforted her, but her words cut too deeply. He knew she was sick and exhausted, but he was exhausted, also. Gradually Duma got up, but she didn't apologize. Indeed, the rest of the day she seemed to go from one family member to another and find some fault with what they were doing. By the end of the day, no one wanted to see her at all.

By the next day they were ready, and traveled back into the forest with some portion of their original group. The rumors had created ill feelings and accusations which had split the larger group into two. When he saw Keen's family traveling with their group, Avid was relieved that he and his friend would continue to travel together. The villagers had not been able to sell or give them much food for the journey because of their own privation. The group traveled through tall oaks whose leaf canopy guaranteed that the young saplings in their shade would grow slowly on a diet of little sun. Maples and beech grew in clusters. Fungus digested dead trunks on the side of the road. The group looked for sources of water and resources to sell at the next village.

There was a small stream near a clearing. Various families set up the usual camp and started cooking. But there was not much to cook. The worst part was that the stream was polluted — some large animals had died slightly upstream. The water was undrinkable, and it was too late to find another camp. Of course, everyone had a water bag with some water, but not enough for cooking, drinking, and washing. The bags held just enough for emergencies.

When morning broke, everyone was hungry and thirsty. Duma finally had a sleep without mosquito and gadfly trouble, and had left most of her anxieties behind with the part of the group that had gone its separate way. Still, one night's sleep didn't make up for weeks of previous sleeplessness. Now hunger and thirst added to her tired misery.

It was harder for everyone to tolerate Duma's criticism and grouchiness as they were unsettled from their own hunger and thirst. Pena had been arguing and crying with Duma for an hour before Avid was even awake.

"You have forgotten the fruits out all night and now they're wet again!" Duma was saying, much too loudly. If she had ended there, all would have been well, but she went on, "And that is just like you, irresponsible and selfish. All you're caring about is your own sleep, and not what we'll need to sell in the next village!"

"Mother!" Pena's tears streamed down her face so profusely that her collar was wet. "I really tried! You have been making it so hard for everyone for at least a week now. It's bad enough that we were being blamed for stuff we didn't do, and the group broke up. But you have been fighting our own family! Stop!" And then she turned away and kicked a pebble hard.

"I want nothing more to do with any of you!" called Duma to Pena's back. Duma then walked into the forest beyond where anyone could see her. She was naturally careful to watch where she was going so she could get back. *But I don't really care. To become rich and powerful, that's why I left my town, married Tavis and came with the group to the forest. So many promises that we would grow rich from the forest!* Finally, Duma sat on a large rock. She did not really notice the forest or its creatures around her, but let her mind swirl in and over itself again and again.

Avid had watched Duma go into a dense area of trees. *I don't even want to go and get my mother. Let her stay where she is until she's normal again.* Avid sighed at his own anger but went about his morning duties as best he could without water, anxious to move on as fast as possible.

A Castle

Duma sullenly returned to the group for the meager breakfast, which hardly anyone could eat — it was only their stock of dried food without water. While everyone was grateful there was anything at all, no one could call that a meal. Packing without water to drink or a sufficient meal, after the previous day of intense travel, meant everyone was easily irritated.

But hours would go by before anyone found water. First, they found something else. Shimmering, sparkling, shining — it appeared that a magnificent city had materialized in the distance. Not everyone saw it, but most did. "A city! A castle!" the voices in the group got louder and more excited. Avid wondered if there would finally be a place they could call home. What a beautiful place!

The vision inspired the group to move faster and with renewed energy, though some who couldn't see the castle continued to grumble. Sometimes the city seemed to be getting closer, but other times it appeared to remain always the same distance away. *Is this the path nectar seekers travel on?* Avid felt his expectations rise, and his awareness of thirst subside.

Duma found new energy to walk upon seeing the castle, but she quickly reached her limit and collapsed. Mohah and Tavis picked her up and gently placed her on some thick blankets in some space they opened up in a vehicle. She dreamed deeply...

What a beautiful castle, Duma thought in her dream. *And it's our home, home at last!* There was a table spread with a feast and drinks of all kinds — the most cooling well water, fruit juice full of flavor and health, and invigorating herbal teas. "Everyone come and eat!" she called in her dream. The whole family sat at the table on elegant chairs. *How handsome Tavis still is, with Mohah and Bron men now. And Sarala such a lady!* Pena and Avid hugged her, and her mother-in-law smiled and blessed her. So many friends were also there, and all ate and drank to their satisfaction.

While Duma only slept for a few hours, the dream spanned many years, as dream time can do. In her dream, Mohah, Bron, and Sarala each got married in the castle courtyard to charming spouses. Mohah and his wife brought their first child home to visit, and the celebration went on for many days. Tavis had found a way to buy and sell without traveling, and Duma saw herself wearing many outfits worthy of a queen. Friends and neighbors, who were both former traveling companions and people she had not yet met in waking life, praised their family and brought gifts.

Life carried on in the beautiful castle. Pena and Avid were grown and courting. Tavis had retired. Duma was planning Pena's wedding. Bron and his wife had twins, while Mohah and his wife now had five children, and Sarala was expecting. The town was full of splendor and opulence. When Duma looked in the mirror in her dream, she saw, indeed, an older face, but a glowing one. Everyone appeared to be glowing and happy beyond measure. Then, in the dream, Tavis became ill, and no healer had a cure. He slowly died, holding her hand, and she cried by his deathbed. "What a good man, a good man! Everything is lost!" Duma cried as Pena held her in a tight embrace.

While Duma was sleeping, the party finally came to clean water in a rushing stream. On the sides of the stream were fruit trees in season, and plants Sarala recognized as having edible roots. Keen and Bron found a clearing where they could set up for the night, or maybe longer. And everyone drank. Tavis took water and fruits to his wife, rousing her from slumber. When she saw her husband still living, she held him for a long time even before drinking. "Oh, I have been so cruel to you. I apologize. I love you," she babbled. Tavis slightly smiled and gave her some water.

After everyone had drunk, washed, eaten, and set up camp, they each gradually noticed that the city and castle had vanished. Some guessed that it had just gotten out of view when they turned, and would soon reappear. There was much discussion about the city that night. But no matter how and where they traveled they never saw it again.

All that Glitters

The place they found by the clean stream with plenty of food became "home" for several months. Sometimes Mohah took Pena and Avid out to find treasure, and one day they encountered something very strange—nearly as strange as the castle in the sky, but this time undoubtedly real.

The group regularly collected stones in the forest. Mostly, these stones were useful as tools, such as for grinding spices. Others were semi-precious for jewelry. Fully precious gems or metals were a rare find. Getting those might mean an end to wandering forest life altogether!

In a little grassy area among the trees, Pena had a basket and was picking herbs to help Bron, as there were not many fruits for her to find, when she saw it in the distance, just a short walk away. Gold! Mohah and Avid rushed over, leaving their piles of wood and stones. Indeed, it was gold. Glittering, shiny, yellow gold. They got out their trail-marking beans and tree-marking colors and walked together towards it. Amazing! "Usually gold is not so obvious," Mohah remarked warily.

Although the glitter was clear from where they were, getting to it proved more difficult than they at first imagined as they had to make their way through thick underbrush. All three ended up using most of their trail-marking beans, and there wasn't really any "path" to mark. Mohah often used his large blade to cut the vegetation, saying, "Careful, get out of the way!" to the younger ones over and over again.

What had appeared at first to be a ten minute distance took

nearly three hours because of some illusion of the reflection, along with having to cut through dense vegetation, as well as twists and turns through the trees... Gradually, as they were walking farther and farther, each wondered how gold could have been seen from so far away. "Maybe the sun was especially shining on it?" Pena suggested. With little water left in their water bags, they finally reached the area. Upon their arrival, Pena's face fell and she looked at her feet. "A swamp! Phosphorescence in a swamp! I feel so dumb..."

"Oh, Pena, it's ok," said Mohah as they all dropped onto large, flat rocks to rest. Because the ground was so moist, large trees trembled just from the vibration of their sitting down simultaneously. "This used to be a lake. Trees and shrubs took it over. Lots of fish, birds, and lizards here," he observed.

"What is phosphorescence, and why did we think it was gold?" Avid looked up at Mohah who seemed to him almost as wise as Tavis.

"No one really knows if it's phosphorescence or not. It's called the will-of-the wisp, and it's usually blue, not gold, as we are seeing it. We see it because there are so many trees shading this area that it's pretty dark even in daytime."

"Sure looked like gold to us," Avid glanced at Pena, and she smiled mostly with her eyes.

"Thanks, little brother."

"Sometimes I think most of the time we spend in the forest is running after wealth that doesn't really exist," Mohah sighed. "Ok, let's go."

"Mohah..." Avid started.

"Yes, little brother?" Mohah touched his head with affection.

"This is not the only magical thing we've seen in this forest, you know."

"Oh, you mean that castle in the sky? That was a mind trick of hungry and tired people."

"And desperate people," added Pena.

"No, I mean something else," Avid said very softly. *Should I tell them? I haven't even told Keen yet...*

"Hmmm... we should get back. I'm sure there are many magical things here, little one. But we're low on water and all we have for our trouble today is a few herbs, low-grade gemstones, and lots of scratches. We really need to get back. Pick something for us all to sing along with you to ease the time."

Avid chose a song he had learned in the last village, "not all that glitters is gold..." and Pena laughed a bit.

Shallow River

One day, they did indeed find real gold, but, in some ways, it proved a worse illusion than the will-of-the-wisp and led to much more trouble.

Sometimes in the forest their group had met other nomadic groups with similar ways of earning a living: collecting valuables cheaply from the forests and selling in the villages. On this day, a warm and sunny one, they met a lone wanderer. He came into the encampment in time for the evening meal, and stayed for several days. The wanderer was dressed in shining long robes that looked like fine silk, and it appeared to be real jewels and gold decorating his clothes and body. He was friendly, helpful, and kind. Later, some said his name was Vitoyah, but others thought it was Vyudaka. Others were not sure at all.

On the second evening after the wanderer's arrival, the entire group gathered after the meal to listen to Vitoyah's stories and advice. He leaned forward, drank deeply of some local fruit juice Pena had prepared, and said, "You are all wasting your time with ordinary things. Do you know the path of the nectar seekers?"

Avid found himself holding his breath and looking around. Was the bee anywhere around?

"If you want real sweetness in life," the wanderer continued, "you need to have religion, which will—"

"We have a religion," Grandma interrupted. "We give regular sacrifices to the lords of the forests, the rivers, the mountains, and the sky. And, we ask the one above all to protect us. This is the religion we have followed for generations."

"What has it gotten you? The real nectar is in gold and opulence so that you don't have to struggle so hard just to eat and sleep. If you have the right religion, you will have the power to attract gold and other wealth with little labor. I will teach you this method just to help you. I don't want anything in return except a place to stay for a few days. I have all the wealth I need from my religious practice."

Avid stared into the woods, beyond the fire, into the darkness, looking for the glow of the bee or whatever that creature was. *Tomorrow I will look for that being again, even if I have to sneak away like I did last time. This man calls himself a nectar seeker like I'm trying to be, but I do not feel the peace, or the understanding…*

The wanderer started describing the deities to be worshiped, prayers, and rituals. Each night he taught them more, and then watched as they practiced, to correct them when needed. Tavis, Duma, Mohah and Bron were especially interested. Sarala and Grandma were content to watch, and Pena said she didn't really care.

After the first day of Vitoyah's instructions, Grandma asked her son to meet with her privately. "Why do you trust this wanderer?"

Tavis shrugged. "No harm."

"I keep wondering what he wants. He says he wants nothing except to share. I talked to my friends in the other families, and some are also suspicious. I think we should be careful."

Tavis looked at his mother as she continued to list her concerns. After perhaps twenty minutes, she seemed to be done. "We'll be careful," he said and stood up. Grandma stood, too, and gave him a hug.

"Maybe he is simply a generous person," Grandma smiled up at her son. "Ok, even if our family is the only one in our group who tries this, we have nothing to lose; you're right."

On the fourth day of the wanderer's visit, Avid found an opportunity to get away, while Grandma was busy with other matters. He took the trail-marking beans and went in a direction where there was not likely to be anything worthy of selling in a village. "Bee or whoever you are!" he said in barely a whisper. "I want to be a nectar seeker. Show me the path."

Avid could only spare an hour going on his own without fear of detection, and in that time he found nothing and no one. He tried the next day, and the day after that. On the seventh day, again he felt the stillness and silence and inner glow, though not as deeply as before. This time, he did not see anything of his guide's form, but he could clearly hear the same voice he had heard that day long ago from the bee, "The ocean of nectar is deeper than can be measured, and it is pure happiness. Others try to make cheap nectar that looks and smells something like the real thing, but that path is like a shallow river full of rocks. You can dive in, but you will break your neck."

The silence and stillness made talking seem like unnecessary effort. Avid was so filled with wonder and peace that he didn't really want to say anything anyway. Yet, a question lingered. *This wanderer tells us rituals and prayers. But, I don't know what to do or where to go, or — anything — to find the real nectar you tell me about. I've decided I want to be a nectar seeker. I think I'm a lot more peaceful than most people since I met you, but is that all there is?*

Although Avid only had an unspoken thought, the being answered him. There was a gentle laugh, like might come from a mother, father, or older sibling when a child does something charming but foolish. "Just sincere desire for truth is enough. Enough for now. Careful of shallow rivers filled with rocks that look like deep clear water."

Avid slowly moved, appreciating the lingering fearlessness and understanding. A bird with a call like laughter sat on a branch of an ancient tree, and the wind blew seeds that fluttered in dancing, spiral patterns to the forest floor.

Again, Avid was able to return without anyone noticing he was gone. Within two weeks, most of the members of the group were following the wanderer's suggestions. Avid participated a bit here and there if his parents were participating and they expected him to follow. His heart and mind were elsewhere, though.

The wanderer had been right — his ritual process brought the group to a vein of pure gold, very near the surface of the river's bank. Some gold was also in the river itself. Naturally they gave a portion of the gold to Vitoyah out of gratitude. Although he had said he wanted nothing, he accepted it with thanks. And the divine bee had been right also. The gold was mostly in and next to a river that was not too far from the swamp where they had found the will-of-the wisp. All the members of the group gathered so much gold that they threw away most of the other material they had gathered previously. Sometimes they had to pan for the gold, and the more ambitious members of the group did often fall into the shallow river and get bruised or cut on the sharp stones there. It was a dangerous place and dangerous work.

Duma was excited, more excited, Tavis remarked, than on their wedding day. She organized everyone in the family, was careful to swear everyone in their group to secrecy about their new religion and the gold, and was at the river every moment she could spare. Usually, she was able to recruit Mohah to help, and they worked together hour after hour. After a particularly difficult day where she got so many cuts that she looked like she had rolled down a rocky mountain, Duma put her arm around her oldest with affection. "This is my dream come true, Mohah my dear." *Now I have the right to be proud! Gold!* "Thank you for being a good son and being here for us. I am so happy with you."

Mohah smiled.

While Avid helped somewhat, he found the excitement about the gold seemed shallow, as if it rested on the outside of a bubble of disinterested curiosity that had been growing within him. The inside of that bubble was a different kind of curiosity: more intense, patient, and yet eager. A longing for a great sea of nectar, peace, and truth.

PART TWO

The City

Storm

It seemed that their wandering days were over, and the castle they had seen in the sky would now be one firmly planted on the ground. Tavis and Duma diligently followed the wanderer's religion, and over the next five years steadily accumulated wealth, enough to eventually buy a house large enough for each of them to have a room and attached bath. They now lived in a grand city. The ocean was a short walk away, and yet the forest—their home for so long—was also close by.

No longer needing to work to earn a living, Tavis tended a large garden in the back of the house whenever the weather allowed, and also volunteered in a program to help youth who had done criminal activities. Sarala, now twenty-one, liked to do most of the cooking, although they had servants who could easily have done so. She also was learning fashion design and a high level of sewing. Her eyes were firmly on a rich young man from a family which had been wealthy for generations. She spent time learning how to read ancient literature, so when the time came for Duma to ask the man's family if they were interested, they would think her worthy. Mohah did some work with the government forest service. He never lost his love for the woods and nature. Pena was taking high level courses, and Avid, now seventeen, was at the end of regular study in the local school. He and Keen were in many classes together, and sometimes commiserated about how they missed their more informal education in the forest. Grandma had her own house built nearby and came over almost every day. She had returned to her youthful hobby of drying and preserving flowers to make wall decorations.

Bron still lived at home, but he was eager to have his own life. He had opened a shop on the main street of the city where he created various types of herbal medicines and cosmetics. "Aren't you satisfied with living off the family's riches?" Mohah asked one day, perched on a high chair in the shop.

Bottles of various colored glass topped with rolling balls were in a glass case. The case had designs of plants and trees etched on the edges. Another case was filled with glass jars cut to reflect light as if they were made of diamond, ruby, and emerald. That case had mirrors inside so it looked like there were repeating thousands of jars. At least twenty cases were in the room, filled with various sizes and shapes of glass or metal containers. The labels looked hand-written. "No, they're printed," Bron had laughed when Mohah had asked.

The walls were painted with such realistic scenes of forest life that Mohah, when he entered the shop for the first time, thought he had returned to the forest. He had told Bron that only the bird songs were missing.

"I don't want to be a dependent child my whole life. I'm already twenty-three," Bron answered. "Hey, look at these creams, brother. Will heal almost any wound in a week!"

"Who's collecting the herbs for you?"

"You remember when we split from the group in that village, because there were rumors about us?"

"Yes, we could never find out who was spreading the rumors, or even what they were saying."

"Well, the other part of our group obviously wasn't with us when we found the gold. They are still nomads collecting in the forests. Keen's brother was in that other group. You remember — Keen and his family came with our group, but his older brother was accused —"

"Was he guilty?"

Bron shrugged. "Doesn't matter. Now, he and his wife and kids —"

"Wife and kids?"

"Yeah, Mohah, wife and kids. Anyway, they and some friends just collect herbs for me now. I'm hoping to start stores in other villages and towns if I can find some partners. We make good stuff that really works."

For a few hours, between customers, Bron showed Mohah many of the herbal remedies and what they were for. Some were based on old folklore, some on research by master herbalists, and a few on Bron's own tests and research. As they talked and went through the cases, abruptly Mohah pointed outside. "What's happening, Bron?!"

The clear, sunny day had suddenly shifted. A fierce wind pushed down on the trees lining the streets so that high branches seemed to bow to its power, almost brushing the ground. Leaves and twigs, sometimes large branches, fell from them. Swirling funnels of tree parts and the bits of rubbish which collect on even well-cleaned streets raced on the walkways and streets. Those who were walking desperately tried to keep their clothing from blowing up or out. Hats seemed to be trophies of the wind, which appeared to laugh as it snatched them from various heads and carried them beyond the owners' reach.

"Was this predicted, Mohah? I had checked with the weather forecasters and there was no mention…"

"I would've stayed home if it was predicted, Bron! I don't have any idea what this is. I hope the windows in your shop don't blow out!"

Through the windstorm, they saw a young woman across the street, looking at their shop. Like the others walking — or trying to walk — she was struggling to keep her footing. The brothers could see people who could hardly take a step forward as if a huge invisible hand kept pushing them backwards. Yet this woman was determined. A little on the tall side, she was slender, yet with an attractive figure. Dark brown hair tinged with natural deep gold had been obviously carefully styled but now scattered across her face and neck, whipping across her body. She caught Bron's eyes even through the flying debris, as she made her way across the street slowly, being pushed back one step for every two forward.

Mohah noticed her looking at Bron, not at the bottles in the shop window. He turned his attention to Bron, whose face was fixed on her, his eyes lit up with a kind of hunger. Mohah nodded to himself. "Ok, what's her name?"

"Vahtya."

He says her name like it's a cool drink on a hot day. "I think, dear brother, that I know why you have started this business."

"I'm going to marry her, Mohah. Just haven't told the rest of the family yet. She deserves a fortune to keep her like a queen in a castle. I want to do it, no matter how hard I have to work. This business will be more successful than that gold we all found."

"Have you told her all this?" Mohah smiled. Bron just looked at her more intently and didn't answer.

Suddenly the wind got so strong that Vahtya was hardly visible. Leaves, dust, and bits of rubbish swirled around her like she was at the center of a whirlwind, or like she was the whirlwind herself. She was then pushed back strongly into the street and lost her footing. She started to fall into the path of oncoming vehicles.

Bron rushed from the shop to save her. He somehow battled the wind to get her out of the way, and then barely escaped getting hit by a vehicle himself.

Gradually they came into the store. "Bad storm out there!" she unnecessarily said as she shook leaves from her clothes. "You have something I can use to clean this up?"

Within a few moments, Mohah wondered if he'd become invisible. Bron had introduced him to Vahtya, and then become absorbed in his conversation with her. When Mohah left the shop, neither Bron or Vahtya said good-bye, or even seemed to notice his leaving.

Owls, Crickets, and Snakes

Gradually even Avid noticed that Bron must be interested in something other than just his growing herbal business. He was rarely home, and was distracted when he was. Avid told Mohah one day that every time he visited Bron's shop, the same girl was there. "But I don't think she works there, Mohah, and she can't be always shopping."

Mohah laughed. "Avid, by this time you must be old enough to know what's going on."

"Oh." *Does attachment for a girl always make a person a bit crazy and distracted? Will Mohah get like that too? And Sarala and Pena with boys?* Avid thought about Bron moving out and having his own family. *Life is so boring—we eat, sleep, find mates, reproduce and defend ourselves. Not really much different from any creature. All kinds of happiness lose their flavor quickly. Even here in this beautiful home in the city we're not happier than we were as forest travelers. What is the point of any of it? Then we die and it's all lost. Life is indeed strange.* While especially Mohah and Avid noticed Bron's changed mental and emotional state, no one noticed Pena and how she was going through something similar. Somehow, she was keeping it hidden, and for reasons the whole family—and others—would know soon enough.

As Bron's romance unfolded, and he finally proposed marriage, soon the family and others in the city tried to tell Bron the truth about Vahtya. The rumors were that she was a heartbreaker, charming men one after another and then leaving them devastated.

Some of her former loves came to Bron and described how she drove them into poverty with her demands for luxuries. If anyone was very strong in condemning Vahtya, Bron simply stopped speaking to that person. *Vahtya may have a bad past*, he considered, *but she would never hurt me when she loves me so much. These people are simply jealous that such a beauty is in love with me.*

Tavis's family had brought great wealth to the city, employing people, starting businesses like Bron had done, and generally spreading the city's fame. While other members of their former traveling forest group had also gotten wealthy from the gold, Tavis's family had by far the most riches. As often happens when poor, struggling families get suddenly rich, Tavis's family — especially Mohah and Duma — regularly flaunted their wealth.

Although superficially he was like any other student, Avid's interest in learning how to be a nectar seeker kept growing within him. He thought about it many times a day. He decided to call it "essence seeking" because the bee-like being said that the real nectar is the essence of life. Maybe his family's moving from struggling nomads in the forest to wealthy homeowners in the city had increased this desire. Though they now lived the success they had struggled for, that achievement seemed to him like a hollow trophy in a display case. He felt life's real questions were not about where to find food, money, or others' appreciation, but to know our identity beyond our body, thoughts and ego. He often looked for his mysterious guide in the forest and encountered the bee from time to time. Once or twice he had tried to talk to Mohah about it, but Mohah would get impatient after a few minutes. He hadn't even tried with anyone else in the family, unless one would count Grandma. He had spoken with her about looking for the essence of life instead of just surviving, and hoped someday to reveal his unusual experiences with his bee-like, nectar-seeking guide. Grandma would say that they were doing more than just surviving. But accumulating wealth in a city or finding goods to sell in the forest — it was all just surviving to Avid. Avid would go after school a few times a week to Keen's place to watch him work on his art. Keen was the only one interested in Avid's search for the nectar beyond the ordinary, and played with the idea of calling himself an essence seeker, as well.

In the library at school, Keen often helped Avid look for books about essence seeking. One day they found a book which gave information that seemed like echoes of the dream Avid had years before, in the forest after he first saw Keen's clay figures. The book was from a school in a place called Acumen. "Here it says we are spiritual beings, moving from one body to another, Avid."

"Yeah, even animal and bird bodies. I remember the aching I felt for sun and water in that dream when I was in a tree body. It was intense."

"I wonder why we can't remember. Why does this life seem like everything?"

"I can remember a bit," Avid said softly, looking away. Then he looked at Keen again. "What more does it say in that book?"

As they read, Keen sensed a connection between the words on the page and his sculptures. It was as if, through hands and clay, he had been trying to ask and answer his questions while growing up, even those he felt rather than said. Now those very questions and answers were on the pages in front of him.

"This book is from Acumen —?" Keen asked. But, the loud bell for class was a powerful interrupter. Keen thrust the book back onto a shelf, hopefully in the right place so they could find it again, and they rushed to their next class.

When Keen went home, he sat outside with clay and a knife for longer than usual, even at the cost of neglecting some work for school. While watching a butterfly emerging from its chrysalis, he captured in clay the moment it started to expand its wings. Just as he finished his sculpture an hour later, the butterfly started its maiden flight. Immediately, a bird swooped down and joyfully made a meal of it. In that moment, Keen decided to join Avid as an essence seeker in earnest. As a fitting tribute both to the butterfly and his determination, he carefully took his sculpture to his studio to fire and paint it.

When Avid got home, the mood was frantic. Doctors and healers were in the house. No one talked loudly or rushed, but tension filled the air. Mohah had been bitten by a snake! The area around the two puncture wounds was red and swollen, and he was alternating between vomiting and struggling to breathe. He had seen the snake moments before, so the healers could identify it and get the anti-venom. Minutes mattered, and Mohah groaned with spasm and agony.

"One would think the forest nomads would be glad to have a forest worker who used to be one of them, Ma," Duma said to Grandma, who had rushed over when Sarala brought her the news. "Mohah takes care of the forest near here and keeps it from being ruined. That way forest nomads can continue to collect wealth peacefully." Duma wanted to put something on the bites, to do something, to do anything, but the healers kept gently but firmly moving her back. *My son, the one who understands the most about… about… everything.* She moved closer to the healers to see better. *Those stupid people who don't appreciate him and did this to him. He is so good, and caring, and helpful.* "Mohah is just trying to give back, after all those years of his own forest life!"

"Ah, you know what envy is, Duma, I would expect by now."

"What do you mean, Grandma?" asked Pena.

"We're rich, sweetie. Very rich. That means we live nicely and don't have to wander anymore in the forests, but it also means others don't wish us well. They wish they had what we have. Envy is a nasty thing. Snakes are so full of hatred that they attack people and creatures who do not harm them. They attack creatures they will not eat. Snakes are full of fear, hatred, and envy. They attack just to attack."

"Is that what happened to Mohah?" Avid asked Grandma. She turned to him briefly and nodded, and then went back to helping the healers.

Avid sat down a bit away from the commotion, as he didn't know what he could do to help and didn't want to be in the way. Tavis came to sit beside him, and silently put his arm around his youngest child. Even though he had recently had his eighteenth birthday, Avid didn't feel too old for fatherly comfort in that moment, and leaned against his father with a sigh. After a while, Sarala came and sat by them. Soon Bron came home, brought by the news, and rushed to Mohah's side.

"Father?" Sarala said quietly. Tavis looked at her and smiled a little. *These are good children,* he thought, for yet another of so many countless times. "That was an uncommon snake, wasn't it?" Tavis's small smile quickly melted back into a straight line. "I wonder if one of the nomads put it where they knew Mohah would be walking. He works so hard to make sure they'll be taken care of, but I know a few of them who think he wants them to stay forest nomads and always worry about money."

"You think some enemy of Mohah's put the snake in his path, Sarala?" Avid's eyes got very wide, and Tavis turned from his children to stare at the healers working on Mohah.

"I don't know, Avid," Sarala answered, "but I do know that he has enemies in the forest. He tries to pretend they aren't there, but we all know they certainly are. The snake that bit him usually stays in thick bush where no humans ever walk. It's the most poisonous snake in the forest, but we never saw one in all the years we traveled there. It stays off of human trails. And Mohah was on a trail near the city. That kind of snake wouldn't be there."

"Why would anyone want Mohah dead or sick? How would that help them?"

"Envy is blind," Grandma said. "It's not logic, children. Looks like Mohah is feeling a bit better. Let's go see if we can help."

It took over three weeks for the bite to heal, and the healers had to remove some of the muscle on Mohah's leg that had died from the venom. There would always be a scar and an indentation in the leg, the healer told him.

Each family member tried to convince Mohah to stop his work in the forest. "I keep the paths clean and clear for those gathering forest riches like we used to do," he repeated to Duma and Grandma for what seemed like the hundredth time in the last few days. "I remember how hard it was for us, and I want to help others who are in the situations we used to be in. I make sure there are no plants on the paths which cause itches and rashes. Every month I go through enough forest area to help people who would be traveling for several months. It's where my heart is."

"But someone must hate you, dear boy," Duma looked at her mother-in-law, hoping for support.

Grandma locked eyes with Mohah, "We want you alive and healthy. And you need to give back for all we've taken. That's true. I know you don't need money. Not yet." Mohah's eyes smiled a little at the thought of a certain young woman. "Or maybe soon?" Mohah tried his best to make a serious face. "Anyway, Mohah, isn't there a safer way you can be of service to others?"

"I love the forest. I grew up there. I feel it's my home. I'll think about it, Mother and Grandma, I promise I will."

That night Mohah decided to go into the forest alone. It would be his first time there since the snake bite. *If I go at night to be helpful, no one will know it's me doing anything. But of course it's too dark for me to be of much good! The irony!*

A bite from a venomous snake is painful and a death threat, so it's not surprising that Mohah, used to forest life for as long as he could remember, kept finding himself jumping in fear as he trekked into the forest. *Do I hear children singing or something else? Is someone following me?* He started to sweat, and sat on a rock. *Oh, just lots of crickets! What's the matter with me?* Mohah finally stood up and looked for an area the half-moon would have lit up enough for him to work. But the crickets kept startling him.

He put on heavy gloves to clear out some poisonous plants that give itchy rashes to most people who touch them. As he worked in the dim moonlight, he felt the inner glow of doing good for others without notice or praise.

"Whoo ooo! Who? Who? Who?" echoed in the trees.

Mohah jumped and his heart started to race. *Who is calling in the forest? Is someone looking for me? Does anyone know I'm here?* "Whoo ooo! Who? Who? Who?" A very large owl perched near Mohah, blinking his eyes and turning his head in ways that seemed impossible. Mohah slowly and carefully, in small movements, turned towards the sound of its call.

"Oh, an owl!" he whispered. *What is wrong with me? I grew up with owls and crickets. Why do they sound tonight like enemies working in the dark, wanting to kill me? I need to act like a man!*

After hours of fretting at the sound of every cricket and owl, every creature running in the forest, and even his own faint moon-shadow, Mohah made his way, jumping at every sound, to his home and his bed, though he did not sleep. He never told anyone of that night in the forest. After that night, however, he decided to do work in the city, and avoid the forest entirely. Months later, the traveling forest groups who had been there when Mohah got bitten — and who had most likely put the snake in his path — moved on to forests farther away. After trying different city jobs, and feeling a bit more confident, he opened a school teaching woodcraft. Students learned how to find and mark paths, recognize useful things such as forest herbs, gems, metals, and types of wood, and avoid dangerous plants and animals. He thus only entered the forests again with his students, and not alone. Grandma introduced him to a lovely young woman, and when he proposed marriage, the family and much of the city rejoiced.

Ceremonies

While Mohah's bride's family did most of the work and covered most of the expense for the wedding, still Duma, Sarala, and Grandma helped for weeks to plan the event and the meal. "Woman's work," said Tavis when Duma asked him for help. She simply sighed, as she knew a discussion would not be fruitful. The biggest problem was deciding whom to invite — and whom not to. One couldn't be too careful, as many people in the city envied the sudden and amazing wealth of Tavis's family and his friends. No one could understand how they got wealthy so quickly, as they had parlayed their gold into greater wealth by selling or trading it in various villages and cities before they brought what they had accumulated to their current city and purchased their fine home. No one in the group ever revealed the religious rituals they had used to find the gold, as the wanderer had instructed them. Suspicions of criminal activities always swirled around them.

After the weeks of planning, and the exhausting day of Mohah's wedding, Sarala announced her own upcoming marriage. Tavis had asked a friend to introduce her to the man she'd been longing for—the son of a long-wealthy family from across town. He was handsome, gentlemanly, and well-situated in his family business. Duma and Grandma felt they had hardly any time to recover from one wedding before planning another. Avid was still too busy in his studies to be of much help. He also spent time daily—though none of his family members noticed—trying to practice techniques of meditation he and Keen had read about in the library, although it was difficult without a teacher.

Avid and Keen regularly met in the library to look for, and study together, any books or articles they could find on nectar seeking or essence seeking. "These weddings are like climbing huge mountains," Avid remarked one day as they closed a book that said happiness is to be found within rather than through external pleasures.

"Mountains with sharp stones, Avid," Keen laughed.

"And lots of thorn bushes."

"Grandma is getting pretty old and yet she's been going with Sarala to every fabric shop in town. How much fabric do they need for one dress?"

"It's not one dress, Avid. They need matching dresses for all her friends. And sometimes the friends don't like the color or the style. They have to try to please everyone and yet do it their own way."

"And the guest list, Keen! Even my father got involved in deciding who should come and who should not come. It had to be a different list from Mohah's wedding, but not too different. It should be a time of joy in the house, but I think we are arguing more than we have for a long time."

"Hopefully not as much as years ago when your mother wasn't sleeping for weeks!" They both laughed at the memory.

"No, not that much, Keen. Still, I don't even like to be home."

"Life is not meant for the happiness available to the animals, but for eternal and unlimited happiness by spiritual realization," Keen read.

They both laughed really hard that time.

Sarala's wedding really did take place high up on a mountain. She and her fiancé had wanted a place with a beautiful view. Some people lived up there, on the outskirts of the city, but there wasn't a hall or any decent place to accommodate the 400 guests. Tavis and his brothers, Mohah and his new brothers-in-law, and many other important people in the city came to help set up tents. For at least a week most of the family climbed up and down the mountain three or more times a day. The sharp stones and thorn bushes Avid and Keen had joked about really were on the path, and more than once a day people got a thorn through their shoe, or had one rip their clothing. Bron didn't help much with the preparation, saying he was too busy with his business, but there was plenty of eye-rolling when he said that. "Business or Vahtya?" Avid heard Duma say to Grandma, but she didn't smile. And, while Pena helped out a lot on a few days, on other days she would just seem to vanish, and no one could find her for hours. "What is that girl doing up there on the mountain?" Duma would say to no one in particular.

Tavis would have let Sarala have her way in everything without even a discussion, but Grandma insisted that the cooking had to take place in the city, and only the finished, cooked items brought up the mountain. Doing things that way limited what kind of food preparations could be served.

At the wedding feast, Mohah's wife announced that she was expecting a baby! Duma and Grandma hugged her, but Avid noticed that when his mother looked away, she also looked exhausted. He heard her whisper to Grandma, "I don't know if I have the energy to organize a baby shower. I hope she has friends who can do it, and that her own mother will help. I'm exhausted." But when guests came to offer congratulations, Duma covered her exhaustion with a beaming smile.

Taxes

Soon after Sarala's wedding, Tavis called a family meeting. "When we spent all the money on Sarala's wedding, we had already paid our taxes."

"Or so you thought," said Duma. *Somehow, we need to hold on to our money.* "Government!"

"Yes. An official from the government told me today we owe a lot more."

"Why are you telling us this?" Bron asked, looking like he had an important meeting to get to.

"We need to cut back on spending for quite a while. I need your help."

Bron stood up and shook his fist. He said, "The government should want us to prosper. Our doing well helps the whole country. I know they need taxes for roads, and schools, and police, but if they take too much they are taking from their own good. It's like they are cannibalistic monsters, eating their own people!"

"We can try and hide our income more," Duma suggested.

"Already doing that as much as I can," Tavis looked down. "Just don't spend much money for a while. That's all."

Duma gave Avid a brief hug as they got up to go.

About two weeks later, Avid came home from school, singing about the mysteries of countless stars. He stopped in the middle of a line when he found his parents meeting with government tax officials. One of the officials insisted on searching the home to look for hidden wealth. He went through everything and found some gold they had concealed long ago. Tavis would take a little bit from the cache when they needed it for emergencies. The tax

collector took the whole stock, at least from that one place. "They only found one place," Pena whispered to Avid. Avid looked at her hard to silence her in front of the tax collectors.

After that meeting, Tavis hardly spoke at all to anyone about anything. He started eating by himself, and spending most of his time alone and outside. Duma started a project of re-organizing the house, and seemed too busy to do anything with anyone else. There wasn't much of anyone else in the house anyway. Bron was always at his business or with Vahtya, Pena seemed to go out at odd times on unknown errands, and Avid was mostly at school or the library.

Avid always remembered the day it happened. Bron came in for supper with his hair a mess, and his clothes out of order. His eyes were red, and his face was gray. "I think the tax officials broke into my store and took cash," he said. For the next weeks there were police officers, court appointments, and lots of people asking questions with no good answers. Bron became obsessed and had nothing more on his mind than the missing cash.

"How much was it?" Keen asked one day at the library.

Avid shrugged. "I try to stay out of it, but I think it was a lot. I'm going to the shop today after school, though, just to be a good brother. Want to come?"

"Sure."

How Avid and Keen later wished they would have chosen another day to visit Bron! When they arrived, they noticed a particularly handsome young man sitting on a bench a little ways from the shop. "Are you from —?" Keen asked.

"Yes, the town through the woods where your traveling party passed through years ago. I'm surprised you remembered me," the man said.

"I look carefully at everyone. I create sculptures and so am used to seeing with an artist's eye. What brings you here?"

"Oh, I've been in the city for a while," the visitor said. "I'm meeting my favorite girl here. Hope to marry her soon. We're working on a business plan so we can have a fancy wedding, and a nice house." He smiled. "Simple stuff that everyone wants."

"Yeah," said Avid. "See you."

Avid and Keen walked towards Bron's shop. Avid noticed Vahtya in the shop, but Bron wasn't there. In fact, no one else was in there. "Keen, I don't want to go inside right yet. Is it ok if we wait outside for a bit?"

"Sure, but what are you doing?" Keen asked, as Avid was moving to a position where he could see into the shop, but Vahtya couldn't see him.

"Shhhh...."

Avid and Keen could see Vahtya take some money out of the store, give it to the man from the other village, and then the two of them walk away embracing each other. "I don't have the heart to tell Bron that his beloved has been the thief all along," Avid said.

The next day, Avid and Keen told Mohah what they had seen. Mohah sighed. "We heard that Vahtya was a heartbreaker, but he wouldn't listen. I don't think he'll believe us about this, either. He'll need to see it with his own eyes. Even then, maybe she'll make some excuse and he'll believe her."

It took a few days for Mohah to find the right time to bring up the situation to Bron. They were sitting in the shop after closing time. Perhaps Mohah should have just told the facts and let his brother draw his own conclusions, but he used some harsh names for Vahtya, and then called Bron a fool. Bron threw him out of the shop.

After that, Avid didn't even want to try to talk to Bron about the whole thing. He simply prayed that Bron would see for himself. Eventually Bron stopped by the store at a time when Vahtya expected him to be in a nearby city. Everything was exposed.

There was a family meeting and everyone urged Bron to take the matter to the police, but he refused. Avid looked at Bron and tried not to cry. Bron decided to move out of his parents' house.

Avid would regularly go by the store just to be with Bron as a brother, but they never talked about Vahtya or what happened. In fact, it took Bron two years before he would talk about her to anyone, and it was ten years before he would find the woman he would marry.

Sage

One day at the school library, Keen introduced Avid to a girl, Sage. Her hair was tied neatly into a simple style, except for some wayward curls near her ears and forehead. Her modest clothes had many embroidered pictures as well as designs woven into the fabric itself. Avid noticed that her finely tapered fingers had calluses on their tips, from repeated use. *Are those calluses from playing a musical instrument or from working with some sort of craft?*

Keen looked at her as if she was a rare and priceless jewel, and then turned to Avid for his reaction. She shyly looked up at Keen and then down to her feet. "Sage would like to be part of our reading sessions, Avid," Keen said. "She and I have been reading some of these same books you and I read, but she wanted to meet you."

"Are you an artist like Keen, Sage?" Avid asked.

"Well, in a way," she answered. "I create with fabric and textiles, and he creates with clay and paint. We are working on projects together. One of our projects has come from the descriptions from one of these books — how the ultimate place doesn't need a sun, moon, or any form of lighting. It has its own light."

"That information was from another book," answered Avid.

"Yes, over there," Sage said, and started to get up to get it, but Keen quickly got the book for her. She smiled at Keen, and Avid felt oddly happy. "Look at this description!"

They all crowded around the book and discussed it for over an hour: "The inhabitants travel through the sky in vehicles made of lapis lazuli, emerald and gold... some residents carried an umbrella and fans…. the white fans moved very gently, like two swans, and due to their favorable breeze, the pearls garlanding the umbrella also moved, like drops of nectar falling from the white full moon or ice melting due to a gust of wind."

"When I read such things, I want to stop everything else and create the scene out of clay," Keen chuckled at his own enthusiasm.

Finally, the school bell rang for class and they all got up. "Hey, Keen, we graduate this year," said Avid.

"Yeah."

"I'm going to miss these times. I feel more and more like I'm not part of the city, or even my family," Avid sighed. *So, Keen may start his own family. And what will I do? We've shared so much, and I told him about my dream of the strange bee, but I never told him that there is more to it than a dream. Even here in the city, I meet my guide in the nearby forests sometimes. I've waited so long that, now, if tell him it seems I need to tell her, too.*

Avid turned to the girl. "Have you been interested in essence seeking for long, Sage?"

"I love to think, to read, and to discover," she said with her eyes alight. "My father and I regularly talk about things that… well, topics I guess most people would call philosophy. My father just calls them 'life talk.'" Sage laughed and Keen's face lit up as if he mirrored her. She quickly noticed his brightness and blushed.

"I like that — 'life talk' — to find the essence of life," Avid said, trying to act as if he didn't see what was going on between the two. "What kinds of philosophy do you explore?"

"Well, you know Keen's amazing clay art of all the forms of life in the forest, right?"

"Oh, yes!"

"Yes, of course you do," Sage looked down and sideways at Keen who was watching her intently without saying anything. "Keen told me how you felt connected with each form of life."

"I could feel that I had lived in each form myself. It's hard to describe. It was an experience of my real self as different from my present body and even mind. When I was in each form, I would feel as if that form was my identity. As I moved in experience from one form to another, I came to understand that my real identity was none of them."

"So, yes, we would discuss the idea of who we are. Our real identity. You know, Avid, in my art I use fiber to express those ideas in color, movement, and texture. It's not quite how Keen does it," and she looked at Keen again from the corner of her eye, without moving her head, "but I'm using my art to make scenes and backgrounds for his sculptures as well as standalone pieces. I hope you can come and see."

"For sure."

Anger of the Hive

After school, Avid went home. It was just him, Pena, and their parents living in the house, but Pena was often not home. She had already finished her education, but had not started a job, and mostly helped out at home. She seemed to have few other interests, yet was rarely around. Whenever anyone asked where she had been, she would just say, "On the mountain." That day, supper came and went, and she had not returned.

"The days are still long this time of year, Tavis, but I'm getting worried," Duma said. Tavis nodded. Duma touched his shoulder and looked into his eyes. "I'm worried. I want to look for her." Tavis sighed.

"Where would we look, Mother?" asked Avid.

"That's the question," said Tavis. "And she's grown now."

"Grown, but still at home and under our care. She may be hurt somewhere. Please."

Tavis sighed again but he got up and put on a jacket and his heavy boots. Avid and Duma got their forest clothes as well. They all entered the woods.

It was late afternoon, but they had taken some lamps, saving them for the moonless dark. "I hope we find her before these are needed," said Duma to the trees. Avid flinched and grimaced at the thought of looking for her in the mountain woods in the dark, even for experienced foresters.

"We didn't tell anyone where we were going, not even Grandma," said Avid when they were half-way up the mountain. "And did anyone bring tracking beans?"

"I did. No need for them yet," said Tavis as he moved away thorny branches, some of which cut through his thick gloves and jacket.

Every few steps Duma called out, "Pena! Pena!" but only birds called back as they were returning to their nests and the sky started to redden.

"I remember all our forest evening meals," said Avid. *I miss those days sometimes. Our life was harder then, though. Always a struggle with no goal.* He was also looking for Pena, sometimes calling, sometimes scanning the area. And all three of them were looking for tracks. "Here! Look!" Avid finally said and stopped. Tavis and Duma came close. Clearly footprints, fresh. "Any of us able to recognize her shoe prints?"

Tavis gave a quarter-smile, nodded, and led the way, following her tracks. Those were often hidden by blown leaves, but the searchers were making steady progress, now leaving tracking beans to mark their way as the sky deepened with crimson, streaked with deeper blue. "Pena!" Tavis finally called, joining Duma.

It was Avid who found her. He had smelled honey and heard bees which had momentarily distracted him, his mind flowing to his mysterious guide and friend in the forest. In his distraction, he started walking towards a very large beehive, and there was Pena, lying on the ground and moaning, with bees swarming around her. "She's here!" he said. He quickly tied together some leaves that would smoke rather than flame, and lit them. The smoke made everyone cough a bit but the bees flew away from his sister.

"Pena! Pena!" Duma became frantic, and Tavis followed silently and grimly behind. Duma picked up Pena's upper body and put it on her lap. Pena's face and arms were covered with swollen bee stings. One eye was swollen shut, and she was slightly breathing. Sometimes she would moan. "We need to get her to a healer fast," Duma looked at Tavis. "Can we carry her down?" Duma looked closely at Pena. *That's odd. Pena's clothing is disheveled.* "Something seems very strange!"

Tavis and Avid started looking around to gather materials to make a simple stretcher to carry her. They would need two long, sturdy poles and then something that would act like fabric. Their years of forest life suited them well, and they knew exactly what would work.

"Hey! There is someone else here!" Avid called to his parents. "He has also been stung many times."

Tavis hurried over. "I know him. He is Lumpatah, Dukha's husband."

Duma couldn't see the man on the ground, but she could hear the conversation. "What is he doing here? I know them. We met them at friends' weddings and parties."

"Yes, I know him," Avid said too quietly for anyone to hear. He turned to his father. "How will the three of us carry two people down the mountain? We can't carry two stretchers and it will be very hard to make one big enough and strong enough to carry both of them." Avid looked carefully at Lumpatah, and, along with Tavis, they tried their best to put him in a more comfortable position. They couldn't stay with him like Duma was staying with Pena, because they had to find materials to build a stretcher. "Funny, he has taken off his socks and shoes. And his shirt is mostly unbuttoned. What were they doing here, I wonder."

"Getting honey," said Tavis.

"Strange way to dress to steal honey from wild bees," said Duma. *At least we have the money and position for a good healer, better than our struggling forest days.* "Pena has no shoes on either. Oh, I see their shoes. Over by that tree."

"I'll get them," Avid scrambled to help.

"Pena has never been really interested in honey. She has never brought honey home," Duma thought out loud. "And why is she here with Lumpatah?"

"Maybe she got hurt by the bees, Lumpatah came to help her, and he got stung himself?" suggested Avid. "At least I'm glad that now that it's gotten much darker, the bees aren't going to attack us. Of course, we're not trying to steal their honey." He allowed himself a little laugh, though he felt really scared and hoped his sister would be ok.

"These are not the kind of bees that sting without reason," Duma said. "For sure these two were stealing honey."

"Hope we can finish while there's light," Tavis said.

Usually the family would have noticed any strange sounds in the forest, but they were so perplexed by the whole situation that they weren't really paying attention. Someone was thrashing through the forest, someone who didn't know how to travel quietly or safely. "Lumpatah!" a woman's voice rang out. "I know you are with that girl! I know it. Where are you?"

Suddenly Dukha came to the area where everyone was gathered. They all went very still and just stared at each other. Finally, Duma spoke. "Oh, Dukha, we had no idea until now. This is terrible."

"That woman—your daughter—is stealing my husband. She will be sorry! I will make her life miserable!" Dukha yelled and then started to cry. "Where is Lumpatah? Is he ok? Where is he?"

"Her life is already miserable," Avid said, apparently to Dukha, but so quietly it's not likely she heard him. "It's natural. When you try to steal someone's honey you get attacked."

With four people to carry the injured, Tavis and Avid now made two stretchers. They were able to carry Lumpatah and Pena down most of the mountain before it got too dark to see anything. Using their lamps, they made it to the healer's.

The healer had them gently set Pena and Lumpatah on two sheet-covered cushions. Dukha, Duma, and Tavis struggled with an internal war between worry and anger. *How could Pena do such a thing?* Duma thought over and over until it became like the chorus of a song.

"They will be all right," the healer said after a while. Tavis, Duma, Avid, and Dukha breathed in relief as if they had been holding their breath for hours. Duma and Dukha collapsed into chairs. "At least their bodies will heal," the healer continued.

"Healing their betrayal of trust of those who love them may take longer," Duma said softly.

Avid looked at Pena's swollen eye. *One should be satisfied with what is set aside as one's quota. One should not accept other things, knowing well to whom they belong.* Avid held his sister's hand carefully, so as not to touch the stings. *Why did she want to love another woman's husband? The bees will protect their honey.* He stood by her side for a long time as the healer plucked out stingers, applied salves to the stings, and dropped medicine into Pena's mouth. It would be a long night.

Python

Once Pena was well, Grandma suggested that she move out of the city. Dukha and Lumpatah were trying to fix their relationship, and it didn't help to have Pena around. Also, Pena was miserable, alternating between crying over losing Lumpatah and shame over what she had done. Grandma spent hours staying with Pena every day doing some housework and crafts together. The problem was that Grandma kept falling asleep. "Ah, in sleep I don't feel any of the difficulties of life," she would say. "And life is full of difficulties."

Duma mentioned to Tavis that his mother seemed to be falling asleep often during the day. "She worked hard her whole life," was his only reply, but Duma kept begging Grandma to see a healer, to no avail.

After some weeks, Duma arranged for Pena to have a job in another city where she could stay with people they had met in their forest life. Although Pena didn't want to leave her family, she was glad to be away from the whispers and open taunts whenever she went out. Duma traveled with Pena to help her get settled. With Duma gone for a month, Grandma temporarily moved in with her son and grandson. Avid helped Grandma with meals and enjoyed their time together.

Avid reflected that the upcoming graduation from school might mean he and his friends would move away from each other. He decided it was time to tell Keen and Sage about his unusual encounters with the celestial bee-like being. He and Keen had shared so much, it seemed wrong to keep this a secret anymore when he or Keen might move elsewhere soon. But, a secret one has carried for a long time gets harder and harder to give up. To muster his courage, he reasoned that the secret he had carried for so many years was not really stranger than a lot of what they had read in the library.

On a gorgeous day when the three of them were eating a picnic lunch outside, Avid took a deep breath and looked at his friend since childhood. "Something I've been wanting to tell you, and, well, you might think I'm making it up, but, you see, well, it started years ago —" He looked at his feet and stopped.

"And —?" Sage asked with wide eyes.

Avid took yet another deep breath and told them both of the first time he encountered his guide and of some of the times after that which had made the deepest impressions upon him.

Keen merely laughed softly and leaned back in his seat. "You told me about some divine bee you saw in a dream, Avid, and you told me with such emotion. I should have guessed. Do you think this being might appear to us, too?"

Sage asked if there was anything in the books like Avid's experience. After a few days of researching in books, she decided she believed Avid and was also curious if she could share in the experience.

Avid suggested that all three of them try going to the places in the nearby forests where he had had encounters since living in the city.

"Have you told anyone else?" Sage asked.

"I have tried but never got past the trying. I have especially wanted to share with Grandma. She would always be honest with me, and I would like to be open with her, too."

"What if you present it as a way she could spend some time getting to know your friends better by being with the three of us?"

"The problem is that she's mostly what my mother calls a practical person. But maybe with my mother gone, she'd be open to it. I'm not sure."

"Please ask her, Avid. It would make me happy if you got to

share this with her," Sage smiled, which meant Keen smiled too.

One day after lunch when there was no school, Avid decided to try and talk to Grandma about the peace and understanding he found when meeting his mysterious guide in the forest, and about the books he, Keen, and Sage were reading. Grandma stayed awake just long enough to hear something that made her curious, she said. She asked Avid to go with her to the forest so they could look for what she called "the magic." Her using the word magic made Avid think of the process they used to find gold, a sour thought, but he hoped that if she saw the celestial bee everything would become clear for her. They made a plan to look for Avid's guide the next day, when school would also be closed and the weather promised to be pleasant.

Mid-morning on the next day as they set out, Avid explained that he didn't have a particular place to go in the nearby forest where he could be sure of finding his mysterious helper, but he liked to sit by a small stream of water that gurgled over rocks and was shaded by trees. All four of them — Grandma, Avid, Keen, and Sage — well-versed in forest craft, sat so quietly that the area soon filled with birds of all sizes and colors. A seemingly plain gray bird walked up through the water, moving as much with his neck as his feet. Suddenly, as the sun shone through a gap in the trees and hit the bird's neck, all four had a collective intake of breath. His neck was an iridescent green, sparkling like emeralds fit for an emperor. A pair of pink and orange birds danced on the other side of the stream, one bird appearing to chase the other. Abruptly, the pursuer fluffed up a large crest of gold and purple. Seeing that, Sage leaned her head on Keen's shoulder, and he put his arm around her. The second bird turned and looked long at the large crest and chirped in reply. Green parrots landed in the trees.

Bird sounds like wind instruments mixed with the percussive thrumming of moving water and rustling leaves, and then the buzzing of bees. As Keen listened, he felt that the sounds were changing to become some sort of symphony different from general forest sounds. He looked at Avid to see if he also noticed, and Avid glanced at him from the corners of his eyes, giving a slight nod. A voice not of the animal world then seemed to mix with the other sounds. Afterward, Sage tried to describe it as human, but it was more musical than she had ever heard a human voice in speaking. "Birds," it said, or almost sang. "Birds are his artistic sense."

Everyone held their breath, and then all went silent. Not only was there silence, but it seemed the stream had stopped flowing. Again, Avid felt that he could move if he wanted to, but that he didn't want to. Keen later described the sensation as a combination of utter relaxation and utter alertness. Sage said it was like a musical concert without sounds. It was only when it was over that they would become aware of why Grandma would not have any way to describe the sensations.

From the area where bees had been gathering honey from some basil plants, a shimmery and brilliant being appeared. While no one could see the being's features clearly, there was a sense of affection and wisdom emanating from it. The musical voice which had described the birds was now louder and more distinct, yet still gentle. It was impossible, Keen would say afterward, to ascribe worldly gender to that voice. "Far away but always very near, within everything and yet outside of everything, moving yet still. The energetic source of all knowledge, happiness, and existence. Seek the essence of life, of everything. Do not delay. What is night for most is day for the seeker, and what is night for the seeker is day for most."

The being disappeared, and the sounds and movement of the forest returned. Sage, Keen, and Avid all felt a lingering sense of euphoria. They looked at each other, and then all three at once realized that they didn't see Grandma. Startled, they stood up and saw that she had fallen asleep on the forest floor where there was a buildup of soft leaves. Around her a vine had fallen, and at first Sage thought it was a snake. She jumped. "Python..." she whispered.

"No, don't worry," Keen said and removed the thick vine that had seemed to be strangling Grandma. "I don't think there are pythons here," he said.

"Years ago, I saw a python eat a large sheep," Sage said. "The snake bites to get a grip and then crushes to stop the heart. After I saw that, my father and I studied all about pythons."

"The heart," said Avid. "You know, Grandma slept through what we saw and heard. It's like a python of sleep stopped her heart from knowing what we now know."

They all sat down again and looked at the stream. "Let's wake her up and go back," Keen suggested.

Grandma was a bit embarrassed when they got back that she had fallen asleep, and as a result she and Avid did not discuss the divine being or any topics related to essence seeking again.

Lion

A week later, Keen, Avid, and Sage finished school together and were part of the grand graduation celebration in the school's sports hall. During the party, Keen told Avid that he and Sage were getting married in a month. They wanted a simple celebration at her parents' house. They had put together a traveling art exhibit and hoped, after the wedding, to journey and seek more of the wisdom they had been reading about in the library. They would sell their art on the way to cover their own needs. Would Avid want to join them? Avid needed no convincing.

Avid spent his time after graduation preparing for a long journey with his friends. He felt he had enough forest craft to survive, both by selling what he would collect and by finding food and supplies in the forest itself. He didn't want to see the world. He wanted to find something beyond the world, although exactly what that was, he wasn't sure and couldn't explain to his parents. Avid and Duma had long discussions, sometimes bordering on arguments, often into the night.

Duma felt panic rise inside her whenever she thought of Avid leaving. One night it really got too much to bear and she asked her mother-in-law to come over and help. "Ma, why won't Avid be part of what we have here? After so much struggle, we are wealthy and have so much respect in this city. What more could he want?"

Grandma shook her head. "I've helped raise that boy. I'll talk to him with you. He's a good boy, though he needs to be more practical. He talked to me about all this essence seeking a while ago. It's all foolishness." She thought about saying something about her trip to the forest to meet Avid's guide, and decided it was better to pretend it never happened.

"We have the essence of life already," Duma paced in the room. *My son is so good in school. He should become a famous scholar or a healer. He needs to choose some practical plan for life. Somehow, I need to get him to think practically and focus on his future. Otherwise, he'll suffer so much.* "Ok, that would be good. Let's you and me and Tavis all talk to him."

Avid sighed when Grandma said they needed to talk. He sat down with her and his parents around a low table in the room that had many of the treasures they kept from their forest wandering days.

"What do you hope to find?" Duma asked Avid again and again. "What about finding a woman to spend your life with and getting a career?"

Avid had heard those questions from her so many times that he couldn't think why he continued to answer them. But, after all, she was his mother and he loved and respected her a lot. Additionally, this particular evening Grandma and Tavis were also in the discussion.

Avid paused and looked at his father who waited and returned the look. "I hope to find the essence of life, the nectar of happiness, what is both within and without, near and far, what is self-illuminating and filled with love."

"No such thing," Grandma said, crossing her arms.

"And a good woman?" asked Duma again. "I've told you about so many prospects—"

"I don't know how to explain this, Mother, but I have only the slightest interest in such things. I was happy at the weddings of Mohah and Sarala, and when Keen married Sage. But I don't want or need that for myself. I feel balanced inside and satisfied."

"If you're satisfied, why are you looking for something mysterious you can't even explain?" asked Grandma. She leaned back and slightly smiled.

Duma leaned forward. *Got him. Oh, please let him stay and be normal!*

Avid smiled and looked at his grandmother with fondness. *It's impossible to explain what I'm satisfied with and not satisfied with.* "Grandma, I don't want a woman, or a house, or a career, or any of these things. I feel satisfied without them. But I want to find the truth of life, who I really am beyond the body and mind. I want to find the source of everything."

Tavis touched Avid's knee. "I don't understand what you want, but I love you. I'll consider your points, son."

The women took Avid's mind in circles, asking the same questions in different ways for several hours. Tavis mostly listened, sometimes nodding his head. Finally, overcome by exhaustion, they all went to bed.

The next day, Duma went to Mohah's house. "Please talk sense into your little brother. He's finished with school, but all he wants is some crazy trip with his friends to find some 'essence' somewhere. He needs a real life. Like you," she said, as she tilted her chin up and smiled with her lips pursed and eyes shining.

"He's talked this rubbish to me before. I told him to give it up. Figured it was a long past, childish thing. He needs to be practical, Momma. I'll go over tonight."

Mohah sat with Avid outside, while their mother sneaked glances through the window. She could hear Mohah shouting. At one point he got up so suddenly that his chair fell over, and he stormed into the house. "Sorry, Momma, I tried. I'm disappointed about what he's doing to himself, to you, to all of us. Can't help those who don't want help. I'll be there for him if he ever regains his sanity. I'm going home." Mohah slammed the house door on his way out.

Avid came in a little later. Duma noticed that his eyes were red and swollen and wondered if he'd been sobbing. *Maybe his tears will soften his hard head.* She sighed and stepped forward to offer a hug, but Avid didn't notice, and quickly went to his room.

After a couple of weeks, the questioning stopped and life

seemed back to normal, except that Avid continued to prepare for the journey and spend time with Keen and Sage, who were living for now in a room in her parents' house. There was no need to set up their own house if they were going to travel soon.

But before they could leave, a great sadness overcame the family. As Avid was going to bed one night, he was sure he heard lions roaring. Lions sometimes wandered in the forest, though they were extremely rare. And if they did come close, they had no interest in humans. *Still, it is a bad omen. A lion's roar means death for some poor creature somewhere.*

Others also heard the lions, and in the morning lion prints and droppings were found in the tall grass and clearings where the forest met the city. Some sheep and goats were missing — most likely to be found in the lions' bellies. For the next few evenings, roars would rattle through the edge of the city, in the area where Avid's family lived. He would look out his window and wonder if he would see their eyes. *All we have can be taken in a moment by death. Lions are scary because they remind us that our life is like water on a waxy leaf of a water lily. Beaded up, ready to roll off.*

Indeed, the lions were an omen for Avid's family. Grandma was getting too weak to leave her bed, and within ten days her spirit left her body and passed from this world. Even Pena came for a few days for the funeral, and the whole family was in mourning. Tavis had been mostly keeping to himself since the incident with the tax collectors, and now he spent most of his days outside, just watching the birds and the sky, with tears on his cheeks.

"Dad?" Avid said, coming up behind him and making sure to make some noise so as not to startle him.

"My son," Tavis said as Avid sat on the ground next to his father. "Best you go on that trip with Keen and his wife. What's her name?"

"Sage."

"Yes. You go and find the essence. Find what can't be lost at death or at the hands of tax collectors. For my own life, I've had so many struggles and joys, but what is really left at the end?"

"I love you, Dad."

"You don't need to stay here. I have your mother, Mohah, Sarala, even Bron." They both smiled. "Find what is true. Don't wait. Life is uncertain." Tavis looked tired from what, for him, was a very long speech.

Avid hugged his father. Then he went to gather all his preparations, say his good-byes, and meet with Keen and Sage. He sang a song of endings and good-byes, wondering if and when he would return.

(Thus ends Jada's story to King Gana. For those who wish only to consider seeking beyond the ordinary, the tale ends here. For those who wish to travel one of the many paths to the essence of life, the story told by Das G. begins as it must have done for King Gana himself.)

PART THREE

Acumen

At the Border

Although Avid had already gone to Mohah's house to say good-bye, only Mohah's wife and young child had been home. Mohah, being seven years older, sometimes seemed part brother, part second father. *I was never able to share my inner desires with him, especially after meeting that amazing guide like a bee. I tried a few times, but he cut me off, or it just never happened. I don't like that we're leaving without saying good-bye. I wish I could do more than that. I wish he would support me.* Avid had, by now, joined Keen and Sage in their vehicle, and they were going towards the edge of the city. Although some of the people they passed knew they were leaving for a journey of unknown length, everyone went about their business as if Keen's vehicle was just one of many on the road. *Everyone is absorbed in his or her own life. We think we are so important and such an influential family in this city, but who cares that we are leaving?*

As the vehicle stopped at a crossing near the city limits, Mohah came up behind them, almost completely out of breath. "Avid! Stop!"

Keen pulled over to the side of the road, and Avid got out to see his brother. "Mohah!" Avid held out his arms to embrace Mohah, and tears started to glide down his face. But Mohah put his hands on his hips and spread his legs slightly.

"What are you doing? All this talk about finding essences or whatever? You're going to leave now, with Grandma newly buried and our parents alone? What about getting a career, a wife, and a house? Are you crazy?" Mohah went on and on, with all the arguments Duma and Grandma had made for weeks until there was nothing more to say, and Avid would not be dissuaded. Avid stood quietly, trying to let Mohah exhaust himself. "He's not going alone, Mohah," said Keen. "We'll take care of him." "You're the same age as he is, and just as foolish!" Mohah yelled, and then regretted it. He had always liked Keen, and didn't want to hurt his feelings.

A dark cloud moved in front of the sun and the temperature got cooler. Avid looked deeply into Mohah's eyes. *What is night for most is day for the seeker, and what is night for the seeker is day for most. He is in the python of sleep, although he appears to be awake. He cannot understand the urge inside me that will not stop, will not let me be satisfied with forest or city.* Avid again tried to embrace Mohah, still without explaining or defending himself. This time, Mohah accepted the embrace, slumped his shoulders, and started to cry. When Avid let go, Mohah dropped to sit on the ground, his head in his hands.

"Please, Avid, don't do this."

"I must, brother," Avid finally said. "It's too important."

Mohah stood and hardened his mouth. "Until you give this up and return to a normal life, you are not my real brother." He quickly turned and walked away. Avid wept for a long time, and then Keen helped him into the vehicle, and they passed to the open road beyond the city.

The sun again appeared and made the road a bright yellow. Avid sang, "Oh, you are the essence of life, the nectar of happiness, what is both within and without, near and far, what is self-illuminating and filled with love; nothing now remains 'mine'. You are my father, my brother, my everything."

Keen had brought a lot of books with them. Many were books Sage had studied with her father from childhood. Some were the same books all three had studied in the school library. Before they had decided to travel, Keen had ordered them from a distant city, Acumen, thinking that after graduation he would like to have his own personal copies. It was to Acumen that they were headed, Keen reminded them. All three took turns driving. When the road was smooth, they also took turns reading out loud from the books.

"Why Acumen, again, Keen? I know we talked about this months ago, but I'm still shaken by talking to Mohah and I need reminding," asked Avid.

Keen was driving and dealing with rough roads, so Sage answered. "It's not just an ordinary city, like where our families live. There are great universities, and also smaller schools, informal. They say a person can find a guide there for anything."

The road smoothed a bit and Keen could relax his grip. The coolness of early evening indicated that they needed to find a place to rest for the night. "There is a small city — or a big village — up ahead," Keen said with a smile. "When I spent time researching our route, I heard that there are places there for travelers."

"Keen, we all know how to live in the forest. Why bother with a city?" Avid laughed.

"Oh, let me spoil my bride!" Keen lightly punched his friend's shoulder.

Sage laughed softly. "Thank you, dearest, but I don't need spoiling. Anyway, the city is just fine." She could not have guessed that the city they were about to enter was not fine at all.

Dutiful and the Witches

A sign as they turned left to the city said: "Entering Dutiful: City of Piety, Responsibility, and Good Works."

"That's the kind of city we lived in and just left!" Avid looked at Keen. "It sounds like a description of Mohah."

"No, not really, Avid. I mean, yeah, everyone in our city pushed Duty and Responsibility, but the only religion there was Gold and Prosperity."

"Isn't that the same thing?"

"Well, maybe, but here in Dutiful I've heard it's a bit different. We can meet some of the teachers here, ok?"

"Ok with me. I'm tired anyway."

They stayed in a friendly home that offered bed and breakfast, and after their morning meal headed toward a nearby building dedicated to study and worship. On the way there, they passed a few groups where people were discussing, or even arguing, about which holy book and teacher to follow. When they arrived at the building, there were a few hundred people there in various rooms, and some guides. "Are you new here?" one of the guides asked the three visitors.

"Yes," answered Keen. "We are looking for direction to find the essence of life."

"You've come to the right place," said the guide. "Most people in the world think life is just about working hard, or they try to find some trick to get more gold than anyone else. Here we have a little bit of a different idea. You see —"

Avid started to open his mouth to speak, and then thought

better of it, covering his mouth as if he had yawned. *Get more gold? What a waste! I remember that wanderer who taught us that religion for getting gold. We got gold, that's true, but I wouldn't say we got happiness or peace. We really weren't any happier in the city with gold than we had been wandering in the forest.* Avid realized he'd missed some of what the guide had been saying and brought his focus back.

"We in Dutiful know there is one Supreme God who is far and near. He has made rules for us to be happy in this world, and if we follow his rules, he rewards us all with prosperity."

As Keen listened, he noticed that the guide's shadow was peculiar. Keen always had awareness of lines, texture, dimensions and shading. Something was wrong. He caught Sage's eye and motioned with his eyebrow, hoping she would see it, too. He tried to appear normal and listen, ignoring what must be some trick of the lighting.

"It's not a trick," the guide continued. "It's learning the laws of the world. We have a holy book here, and some rituals to do, and you can see that we all become happy."

"Happy in what sense?" asked Sage. "We also want to connect with the Divine who is far and near."

The guide smiled broadly at them. It seemed to Keen that his smile would stay frozen for a long time. "Wonderful, wonderful. Come this way," the guide responded. He led them into a library where a class was taking place in part of the room. They went through there, to an office. "Sit down here, please. I think you'll want to become a firm adherent of our beliefs and practices. Yes, yes, those who want the One God who is far and near. You have come to the right place. See, this world is given to us by God for us to enjoy in accord with his laws."

Sage sucked in her breath so hard and fast that she surprised even herself. She now saw clearly not the guide's shadow or the lighting tricking her eyes, but someone standing behind him. He seemed completely unaware and continued to speak about gaining worldly pleasures. As Sage gave more attention to the shadow, she could make out a face which was beautiful beyond description, yet somehow grotesque at the same time in a way that puzzled her. Sage felt her attention pulled into the being in a kind of intense fascination. As she lost track of the guide's words, the shadow being's eyes started to glow. Its clothes were made of pieces of gold coins. Beautiful homes rested in its hands. All sorts of luxuries swirled in its clothing. Sage felt those clothes envelop her mind. She then seemed to be in a grand palace, dressed in fine silks and jewels, with gourmet food and many servants. The room was full of people praising her, giving her a sense of being lord of everything. Sage felt frozen in a kind of curious fear as if she could not avert her eyes back to Keen, but she did poke him, and he grabbed her hand tightly. She wondered if he was able to see the being also. Suddenly, Sage became aware again of what the guide was saying, as if a spell had been broken.

"And then, after death, go to heaven," the guide continued.

As soon as the guide said those words, the creature vanished. Sage and Keen felt a release of tension, and he let her hand go. She leaned into him.

"And heaven is what, exactly?" asked Avid.

"There is a group that says heaven is like a perfect version of what we experience here. As I explained, of course, life here becomes perfect if you fully believe our creed and follow our rituals. You don't have to go to heaven. Real perfection after death is to gain total freedom, to be saved from all suffering."

As the guide spoke of gaining salvation and liberation, this time it was Avid who became aware that something was strange. He first felt, rather than saw, a change in the energy of the room. Gradually he realized that the area behind the guide was bright as if a strong light had turned on behind him. But, a feeling of unease filled Avid, growing with every word the guide said about how after death they would merge into some sort of peaceful bliss. The light now had a form, beautiful yet terrible. Gradually he could see a kind of face, something like a human but with eyes like suns, burning to look at. The being was whispering, "you have earned your freedom," over and over again. Avid found that he no longer could focus on what the guide said as he felt his sense of self was melting. Although the being was full of light, it was not the friendly and reassuring light of his bee-like guide. It was hot as if it would dissolve all identity into nothingness. Yet it promised rest from all troubles. Like the temptation to sleep overcomes those who are very cold, Avid felt himself losing his will to keep any drop of his individuality — even his yearning for the essence — to slip into a vast sea of energetic light. He quickly looked at Keen and Sage, but they seemed strangely tired and unaware of what he was experiencing. "I see," said Keen to the guide.

"So," the guide went on with enthusiasm, "our beliefs are that there is one God, Lord of All and creator of everything."

The brilliant being vanished and Avid shook his whole body slightly, much as a dog would do when coming out of the water. He blinked and listened again, as much as he could.

The guide pointed to a table, "Here is a picture of God's one true prophet who lived here long ago and taught us what we follow. Here's the book of his teachings. Here's another book of our prayers and rituals. You just believe that our creed is true, and you denounce other religions as false. Then you pray according to our book at regular times as explained here, and do your best to live according to the rules."

"Rules like—?" Keen asked, in a much quieter voice than usual.

"Don't steal. Be faithful to your spouse. Don't kill. Try to please God, and you'll have a prosperous life full of wealth, power, and happiness."

"Well," Avid said to Keen with some effort, "it's certainly better than the magic stuff that the wanderer taught us to get gold."

"Yes," answered Keen, gradually gathering his energy and addressing Avid and Sage, though the guide was listening, "there were no rules of right behavior in that system. I mean, no rules about being a good person. Of course, the villages and cities had rules like that just as a practical thing so we can live together in groups. And the wanderer only talked about gold in this world, not of a heaven or some sort of salvation."

Keen continued, now looking directly at the guide, "You said we have to denounce other religions as false. Does everyone in Dutiful follow this same holy book and prophet? On the way here, we passed groups arguing about this point."

"The others are false systems you need to avoid or renounce," the guide said with some force. "Unfortunately, here in Dutiful there are a number of groups like that. If someone appears to be so-called dutiful in one of those systems, it's like breaking all the actual rules. We have the one true path."

"We'll take your books and talk about this among ourselves," said Sage flatly. The guide gave each of them copies, which they paid him for, and they walked outside.

"Did you —?" they all asked each other in unison and then laughed a bit nervously. "What was —?" they said again.

"Let's go back to the home where we stayed last night," said Avid. "I feel exhausted."

The others nodded, and they walked silently on a different route from the one they had taken. On the way, they passed a number of other places of study or worship where they were invited in. With hesitancy they entered each place and listened as the guides said essentially the same thing—they had the one true holy book which required renouncing all others, a prophet who lived long ago, specific rules to follow, and some reward after death of either greater worldly happiness or some sort of oneness with energy and freedom.

In one of the places, Keen was sure a picture on a wall turned into the coin-covered entity, and in another Sage saw the sun streaming into the window become the sun-eyed being Avid had seen. In yet another place, Avid saw a cat become the coin-covered entity. After each time one or more of them saw either of the beings, they would start to discuss it with the others, but then stop. Everything was almost too odd to believe what they were experiencing, and, anyway, they felt their minds to be in a kind of mist or fog.

Finally, they reached the home of the family they were boarding with and each collapsed into a chair. They sat in stunned silence for many minutes. "Did you—?" they all asked each other in unison yet again, and then, yet again, laughed a bit nervously. "What was—?" they said yet again, and this time they all laughed so much they couldn't stop. "Like you sometimes do when you are really scared," Sage would say later. Finally, Keen took a deep breath and stood up. He paced the room for a while, sat down again, and then described what he had seen. His description encouraged the others who shared their experiences. All afternoon they skimmed through the books and material they had bought or collected at the various places to try and make some sense of what was happening. They thought maybe the coin-covered being appeared when people talked about how God would bring them prosperity, and the sun-eyed entity seemed to have something to do with them talking of gaining freedom from worldly troubles through dutiful action.

"At least that's what I think," Avid said.

"Yeah," mused Keen. "It's like those strange beings were affecting the people we were with, but those people couldn't see anything strange themselves. You think those entities were warning us somehow?"

"I'm not sure," Sage said slowly. "They seemed to be putting people into some sort of enchantment. I—I sort of felt like I was under a spell, too."

"Yes, you are right, now that I look at it that way. I was able to resist a bit, but it did seem like some bewilderment has covered my brain. I don't want to stay here long," Keen said with some force.

"It's interesting that each group strongly denounces the others, and yet they have so much in common," Sage said.

"I don't think the essence is found in any of these, Sage," said Keen. "From all our study before coming here, the problem is something we can see in just a few hours. I mean, it's great that they seek God who is far and near, and it's great that they say they want to please him. So, in that sense, they are dealing with

the essence. But I don't think there's any love here, or anything we can call joy. And peace?"

"Just asking God for ordinary prosperity and power is missing the point," Sage said. "And they clearly say that they earn prosperity—or salvation—through their following of a belief and rules."

"Ah, that's the difference between Dutiful and the city where we lived. These people are really serious about following some system. In our home city, such things were more like a side part of life."

"Do they really want to please God here?" Avid asked. "If someone wants to please me for the purpose of getting something from me, do they really want to please me, or just manipulate me?"

All three thoughtfully nodded in agreement. Then Sage jumped up, "Oh, that's the coin-covered witch!" she sat back down. "Did I just say 'witch?' Could they be witches?" She started to pace. "And... the bright one—? Who is it?"

Keen suddenly got up also, walked over to where he kept his things, and started going through his books. He found one and turned the pages. "Ah! I know! Here, listen to this: 'The desire for salvation is a demoness because its reference point is oneself. Even though essence seekers become liberated from confusion and difficulty, liberation is not at all their goal.'"

Keen put the book away. "I want to leave soon," he reminded them, "but we need to stay one more day to earn some money in order to continue to Acumen."

Sage shivered. "I wish we could leave tonight. If we have to stay here another day, I wish I knew how to interact with the locals without also meeting those two demonesses, or witches, or whatever they are."

Avid spent the next day walking around Dutiful on his own. He met many guides who were training people in having a happy family, being caretakers of the planet and their possessions, and being good to others. He would sometimes sit and listen to their talks, or join people in prayer. Several times he encountered each of the witches — if that's what they were — and then he tried to convince himself that he didn't want their allurements. Doing that helped a little, but he kept stopping to rest and read from books he had brought, trying to calm the repeated fear and shock from seeing them. The city was clean and orderly, and most people seemed friendly as long as he didn't discuss a path other than theirs, or mention that he planned to go to Acumen. Locals would try to talk him out of going, saying those in Acumen were impractical people trying to run away from responsibility. Avid later joked to his friends that his family had already granted him immunity to such warnings.

There were still police and jails like in his own city, Avid noticed. *I guess not everyone in Dutiful is dutiful,* he considered ruefully. *And even the dutiful ones are not yet selfless. Yet each of the guides here, in each of the religions, is doing something worthy. They are teaching something better than what is understood by most of the people in our home city, or in many of the villages we passed through as I was growing up. They have something useful.* As he was thinking, he came upon a group they had met the day before along with the coin-clad witch. *I don't want to see her yet again.* He started to cross the street as soon as he could feel that the witch was there, and then decided to face the situation differently. He stopped, and, this time, instead of focusing on her while trying for indifference, with great difficulty he turned his attention from her to the people she hovered over.

Avid tried to connect with the feelings of the people in the group he was watching. He could sense their yearning for something beyond ordinary life like a seed underground reaches towards a sun that is felt yet unseen. Their yearning competed with desires for wealth, power, or freedom, and they were under powerful spells for those goals, but yet their yearning lived. He could feel it akin to his own yearning. Admiration filled him. He felt like a fan at a sporting event, cheering his team to a hoped victory even when the score indicated only defeat. *I love that they are trying to bring themselves and others to the One who is far and near. Even if their motives put them under an enchantment. For now. A desire for the essence — I would hope — can eventually shatter enchantments.* As he thought this, his heart moved deeper in connection with the spellbound people, from admiration and hope to warmth and peaceful joy, much as he had felt when meeting with his guide in the forest. In that moment, he completely lost his fear of the witches. They became merely a curiosity. *I wonder if all these people go to some heaven or salvation when they die, and if those rewards are really eternal like they claim... or are their hopes for such things only enchantments also? Oh, Grandma, where are you? I miss you.* Avid crossed the street, went to a park and watched some city pigeons to quiet his thoughts.

When Avid returned, Keen and Sage were counting the money from sales of their art. He told them of how he lost his fear of the witches. "I hope *I* can learn to love the people here in spite of their demons," Sage said.

I need to contribute something, thought Avid as he helped count the money. *In the next city, I will do something for sure.*

"Avid, you could teach forest craft if you like," Keen said without looking up, as if reading his thoughts. Avid smiled.

The next day, after breakfast, they left for Acumen. Avid could hardly contain his anticipation. *The place from which we got so many of the books we studied!* That Acumen would far exceed his expectation was something he could not have imagined.

Guide to Acumen

The road as they got closer to Acumen was lined with trees which created a canopy to give welcome shade. The three felt like they were traveling through a natural tunnel. Gradually, the road curved up into the foothills of several mountains. The morning sun lit up lakes at the mountains' feet. It looked like there were diamonds, like millions of sparkling boats, rocking on the water, while the tops of the mountains seemed to have been dipped in gold. As they rounded a turn, Acumen came into view in a valley, and the road started a gradual descent toward it. From their vantage point above the city, they could see it was clearly a very different city from either Dutiful or their home. The buildings were not very tall, and the city spread out far, interspersed with agricultural land. There were many parks and ponds throughout.

Right at the city's entrance, there was a welcome center with guidebooks, maps, exhibits, and guides. "Welcome, essence seekers!" smiled an older woman as the three young travelers entered the center. They smiled at her and then at each other. "Please call me Gurvi. That means teacher — a lady teacher. That's not my given name, which is Sara. Even Sara is short for my whole name. But everyone here calls me Gurvi."

"Oh, in one of the books we read, a wise man called his mother Gurvi," Sage said, looking at Keen.

Gurvi nodded as if she knew the book well. "What do you seek in Acumen?" she asked.

"We hope to find the essence of life, the nectar of happiness, what is both within and without, near and far, what is self-illuminating and filled with love," said Avid.

"Ah, the One and True. He who is called God in the world," she replied and motioned them to a table with maps and guidebooks. "Here in Acumen you can choose from the paths that truly lead to the essence. For what purpose do you seek the essence?" She smiled and relaxed, as if she had all the time in the world for their answers.

"I... I'm not sure," said Keen. "I think what I want most is to know the why and the how of everything, every species. I want understanding."

Sage looked down at her hands on the table while Keen was speaking, and then said, "I also want to understand."

"Do you want only to understand?" Gurvi looked deeply into Sage's eyes.

"No, I want more than to understand. I want deep wisdom. At least I think I do. I'm not really sure. In what I read, it kept saying the highest way to the essence is to serve with love and devotion. I'm not sure I know what that means, and I think I already love —," Sage blushed and looked first up at Keen and then down to her lap. "I, I, I mean, well, um, I mean I do already love. But is love of the essence the same as what we usually call love? Is it deeper? I want to experience that love and find my true self."

Avid smiled. He turned to Gurvi. "My desire is more basic than what my friends want." They smiled at him. "When I went through what I came to call the Forest of Material Enjoyment, we experienced the shallow rock-filled rivers of magic, the thorny paths on mountains of fancy ceremonies, the mosquitoes of enemies, the false dreams of castles in the sky, and the pain of misguided romance like dust storms and bee attacks. I'm tired of the disturbance of my mind and senses. I want peace."

Gurvi nodded, seeming to digest the words. "I see that none of you want wealth and worldly happiness." They shook their heads. "Some of those people come here also, but most of them stay in the cities, villages, and forests of the world. Some go to Dutiful where God is also worshiped. We love the guides in Dutiful, but our purpose is different."

I felt love for the guides there also, but I didn't want to stay. Avid looked at Gurvi with a sense of kinship. "What do you suggest we do in Acumen?" he asked her.

"Here is a map of the schools," she opened up one of the many maps by her elbow. "Over here on the western side are the Knowing Connection schools. There, they teach how to find the essence by gaining wisdom. Mostly they study philosophy and discuss the nature of truth and illusion. They are primarily interested in the self-illuminating aspect of the Divine, though they can find the complete understanding also in time. You'll notice lots of libraries in their area." She continued. "In the east, there are the Devotion Connection schools. They discuss and study the activities and personality of the One filled with love. I think they have the most fun there, with lots of singing. Many also include dancing. Their area is filled with places of worship. They also study philosophy, meditate, and work hard, though. That book you talked about, Sage, is from one of the Devotion Connection schools."

"There are more than one of each kind of school?" asked Keen, surprised.

"Oh, yes, certainly," chuckled Gurvi. "Then, in the south there are the Action Connection schools. What they do looks a lot like what is taught in Dutiful, except the purpose is not some heaven here or anywhere in illusion. They work, and then sacrifice the fruits of their work for the sake of connection to the source... Those are popular schools for people who graduated from what is done in Dutiful, though they're not so attractive to anyone who skipped Dutiful. Some people there are looking for the Divine as self-illuminating, some as the Supreme Soul within, and some as the complete loving being. The Action Connection quadrant looks like its own city within the city as there is so much variety. Oh, and in the north are the Mastery Connection schools. Not as many people go there, because their curriculum is much harder. Or," she paused and laughed, "a lot of people go there, but not many stay. They are contemplatives. They mostly meditate and gain mastery over their bodies and minds. Their goal is to see and feel the Divine within themselves, though they also can attain the complete. While all the parts of this city have much natural beauty, the Mastery Connection quadrant especially connects people with nature."

"Here are guidebooks from the different schools," Gurvi motioned to an area in the corner with shelves and tables. "There are snacks and drinks there, too. You are welcome to stay until closing time." And that's exactly what they did.

Acumen and the
Fortune Teller

The three young travelers found a small place in Acumen which they could rent month to month or even week to week. They also arranged for a local shop to sell Keen and Sage's art, and a studio to work in. Avid made an agreement with a local teacher to teach forest craft in his classroom in the afternoons. They decided to try out at least one school in each of the four quadrants, and spend at least a month in Acumen, and probably more. So, they first spent a few days becoming familiar with the city.

The layout was a grid, with avenues going one way, and streets going in the other direction. The avenues' names were colors on the light spectrum in order, and the streets—of which there were far more than avenues—were numbered. Everything was thus easy to find. The avenues were broad, with five lanes in each direction, and a middle section of grass, trees, flowers, walkways, drinking fountains, and benches. On the sidewalks on each side of the avenues there were also benches and various fruit trees evenly spaced. The streets were narrow, with one lane in each direction. There were trees on either side, filled with fragrant flowers. The trees grew together over the streets, forming a canopy. As Acumen was in a valley, the weather was always pleasant, and thus the flowering trees were planted so that at all times of the year some of the trees were in flower, spreading their fragrance through the city. Every five blocks there was a park with a pond, walkways, and play areas for children. A deep but fairly narrow river flowed through the middle of the city, coming from the surrounding mountains. There were several bridges, each of a different design, across the river. In some sections, there were grassy or sandy beaches along the river where the residents could swim.

As they sat on one of the grassy beaches to eat a picnic lunch, a tall man walked past them, in flowing robes with a mat rolled up under his left arm and books under his right. He chose a flat spot and unrolled the mat. Sitting upon it, he put the books on the mat, and took out a sign. "Your fortune told here" the sign said. Sage giggled. "Who believes such people?" she asked and pulled her mouth into a tight smile.

"Oh, let's have some fun," Keen poked her gently on her upper arm. "When we finish our lunch, let's ask what our fortune is."

Avid rolled his eyes and Sage giggled some more.

After scattering the crumbs from their meal to the waiting birds, Keen approached the fortune teller while the other two stood a bit behind him. "What is our fortune?" Keen asked, putting a coin at the man's feet.

The fortune teller looked long at Keen's eyes. "Please sit down," he said at last.

Keen sat, and, after perhaps a minute or two, Sage shrugged and sat down also. Avid looked around, as if someone who knew him might be watching, and then sat down also. The robed man took each of Keen's hands in his own, to look at Keen's palms one after the other. The whole process seemed to Sage to take a very long time. The man several times opened one of his books to find something and then turned back to Keen's hands.

"You have inherited a great fortune," the robed man said at last. "But because your relative died in a far-off land, you never knew about it."

Keen's eyes widened and Avid shook his head.

"Your relative hid the treasure here as he had no time to get it to you."

"Here at this beach?" Keen said lightly.

"No, somewhere in Acumen. But the treasure is guarded. Take care for elephants in musth, a hornet colony, the nature spirits, and a coiled snake. Three are very difficult to avoid, but one, if you are very careful, will step aside and, then, with a slight touch you can find your treasure."

"Thank you," said Keen politely, thinking his parents would be proud of his manners. He stood, and the others stood as well. They walked back to continue their tour of the city. "Did you have fun?" Sage asked Keen, with light sarcasm.

"Entertainment of a sort, I suppose," he replied, "but not the best use of a coin." He sighed.

As they again entered a main avenue, they noticed that the buildings were mostly of old carved stone, each intricate works of art. The main building of each school—and there were hundreds of schools, dozens in each section—was made of a combination of various colored marble put together to form scenes related to the history and focus of that particular school. Usually, the school's name was permanently part of the building, formed with pieces of colored marble. Many of the residential buildings seemed like works of art, brightly colored and intricately decorated. Most residential buildings had gardens with fruit trees and vegetables, and, on the outskirts of Acumen were fields of grain, along with large pastures filled with cows, sheep, and goats. People worked the fields with teams of oxen or sometimes horses. They also saw working elephants bringing in loads of timber from the forests.

The economy of Acumen was tightly connected with the schools that dominated it. Various schools operated medical facilities, libraries, and so forth which the public paid for. Most residents had attended one or more of the schools, and many were current students or professors. Some were both student and professor if they were in a higher division. As each of the schools aimed toward the happiness of finding the essence of life and source of all, almost everyone in Acumen considered him- or herself an essence seeker. All of the schools had places for worship and meditation, and also there were many other such places throughout the city that were loosely associated with schools in the sense of using the same philosophy and practice, but they were not under the control of the schools.

Avid, Keen, and Sage decided that, since their stated goals were understanding, wisdom, and peace, they would start with the two quadrants which focused on those: Mastery Connection and Knowing Connection. Keen wanted to try Mastery Connection first just to, as he put it, "take up the challenge of the most difficult." What he didn't say — and even Sage didn't know — was that he had been trying for some time to put into practice some Mastery Connection methods he had read about back home, and wanted to meet some teachers to go deeper.

"And maybe you'll even find some hidden treasure!" Avid said.

"Oh, quiet!" replied Keen, and they started to wrestle on the rug as if they were young boys again in the forest.

By the next morning, not even Keen gave the slightest thought to the fortune teller's words.

Mastery Connection Schools and the Snake

After a week of settling in, becoming familiar with the city, and establishing a source of income, Keen, Sage, and Avid went to a restaurant in the Mastery Connection area for lunch. The food was tasty, but extremely simple, and frankly, even a bit austere. But what it lacked in richness it more than made up in effect. After the meal, they each noticed a feeling of lightness in the body and clarity in the mind. "It's as if I have double the physical energy with no need to expend it on doing things," Keen remarked.

"I feel like colors are sharper and sounds clearer," answered Sage. "What designs I could make with the yarns I got the other day!"

Keen looked at his wife with shining eyes. "The beauty of this place is an artist's dream," he said only to her.

They walked, or almost glided, as Avid called it, to the library and information center in the Mastery Connection district. The buildings here looked particularly ancient and mysterious. Oil and clarified butter were the fuel for lamps throughout, and paths even inside the buildings had small bridges over ponds with shimmering fish. The buildings facilitated cool and refreshing breezes which brought the smell of various flowers. "I feel like I'm on a different planet," Avid mused after some time.

In the information center, there were guidebooks from over 100 schools. Some focused on releasing and controlling subtle energy in the body. Some were mostly about movements of air within the body, and where that energy concentrates. Others emphasized gaining powers such as healing others by touch, telling the future, and even levitation. Some schools emphasized manifesting whatever one desired. Avid put all those guidebooks to one side. "All of these seem too much like the magic that the wanderer taught us to get gold. We got gold, yes, but we ended up with a similar life, similar problems, only in a fancier house. Water is water whether in a tin or gold cup. We certainly didn't find anything I would call happiness. It certainly isn't the essence of life or the nectar of boundless happiness."

Keen showed them the back of a brochure. A painting showed a person charming a large, coiled snake, getting the snake to open its mouth. The next picture was of the uncoiled snake eating the person, and the last picture of the person inside the snake, both glowing in a rainbow of colors. "I can't make out what this means," he shrugged, and set it aside.

"This one is about how to find nectar in the back of the mouth through moving energy in a subtle whirl there," Sage said as she looked at a brochure.

They all laughed.

"Not that kind of nectar," said Avid.

"Oh, I like these," said Sage. "Here are about a dozen schools that teach a mastery method of getting a loving relationship with the one who is 'far away but always very near, within everything and yet outside of everything, walking yet not walking. The energetic source of all knowledge, happiness, and existence.'"

"What is their process?" asked Avid.

"Well, each one is a bit different, but all seem to have some sort of meditation on the Divine as supremely personal and loving. Here, look them over."

Keen and Avid moved closer, and the three of them looked together.

"These five seem somewhat mechanical," Avid said after some time. "They are working with the breath, or subtle energy centers in the body, the mind, and sometimes a release of coiled energy. Keen, those snake pictures are symbolic of that coiled energy, I'm pretty sure. Some of them focus on sitting postures also. Some use physical movement like spinning in circles. A lot of them explain their science in great detail."

"Oh, here are three I would like to visit," said Sage finally. "While each of these three use different methods, all have the goals of wisdom, peace, and realization of one's ultimate identity. This one is about how intentional meditation becomes realized contemplation. I'm not sure what that means." She slightly frowned. "And they all make a strong point about gaining a vision of the Soul of the Universe in a very personal sense." Avid and Keen agreed with her choices. There was time that day for them to walk through all three and decide where they would attend a few classes.

Taking copies of those three guidebooks, they left the library section and started to walk through the Mastery Connection schools. "After so many years of discussing, studying, trying on our own…" Keen said with great wonder, "…we are in this place beyond anything I imagined." The entire area seemed like a huge park with fruit and flowering trees, running streams of water, and clear ponds or lakes filled with lotuses, lilies, and water birds. There were groups of people doing various exercises and breathing procedures. In various places people were gathered in classes, or sitting in solitary meditation with eyes half-closed. Many of the people meditating looked to be in a deep trance and appeared to be glowing with a beautiful effulgence. Sage's eyes opened so wide in amazed appreciation that she barely blinked.

The three friends signed up for introductory classes in the Dhyana School, (*dhyana* is the penultimate stage of meditation, the brochure had explained). For the next two weeks, every day they all had classes in how to calm the mind by focusing on a form of God along with a vocal or mental chant, mantra, prayer, or holy name. Keen seemed especially adept at being aware of his energy centers and the flow of breath while repeating a mental prayer like a chant. Avid struggled with restlessness of mind and body, and Sage felt she could most easily keep her focus on her heart but not in any other energy center. Their introductory class had over 200 people, and there was a teacher for every five students. Keen's teacher often took his group up to the mountains, where they would meet experienced meditators from various mastery schools. Some lived there in caves or simple dwellings, and some lived in the city but spent many hours there.

Near the end of the two weeks, on one of those excursions, Keen's teacher introduced his students to a group of advanced Mastery Connection practitioners from a variety of schools. The meeting had been pre-arranged so they joined for an outdoor picnic. One person demonstrated how she could levitate, move objects, tell what others were thinking, and bring objects from distant places. Another could instantly produce a feeling of peace and euphoria in others by his touch. Everyone in the group claimed to be able to keep his or her mind completely still and focused for many hours a day.

One man spoke about the coiled snake energy and how he had gotten this energy to uncoil and open its mouth. "Is it really like a snake?" Keen asked.

"Ah, it's a beautiful snake," the man replied. "I can show you. Be careful! Some who claim to show you cannot coil it again and, if you are not ready, there are ill effects. I can uncoil yours for some moments, open its mouth, and then put it back into a sleeping coil again."

Keen looked inquisitively at the teacher, who slightly nodded. "Ok, then," Keen replied.

As everyone watched, the man instructed Keen to sit in a particular way across from him. "This snake energy is a great treasure we all have within us," he said as much to the group as to Keen. The man closed his eyes and breathed with long breaks between inhale and exhale. He then touched Keen's lower back. Keen shivered as if he had gotten a strong static electric shock. Avid felt sure he actually saw a large snake uncoil from Keen's lower back, slither up his spine, and open its mouth.

"It's swallowing me," Keen said in a voice not clearly expressing joy or distress or wonder. Sage sat down and hoped she would not collapse. The teacher and the man working with Keen looked calm, so she tried not to worry.

"I can bring you out. Do not fear," the man said. After some minutes the man again touched Keen's lower back. Avid again thought he saw the snake, this time curling back into a coil and going to sleep. Keen opened his eyes. The man smiled.

"Well?" Sage asked in a voice that sounded especially squeaky to her.

"Strange, awe-inspiring, intense," Keen replied slowly. "I felt like I lost myself."

"Yes, that is the point," the man said. He slightly bowed, and walked away from the group.

Keen went over to his wife and put his arm around her shoulder. He whispered into her ear, "I do not want to lose myself."

The teacher asked the other advanced practitioners to explain the results they achieved. "I am not participating in this world," a young man replied. "I am only an observer. In my heart's energy center I can see myself as a pure soul, a part of the Soul of the World. I revere him and worship him. I am always filled with peace and expanding joy and want nothing in the world. If I want, I can unleash subtle powers, but I'm not interested."

"What is your practice?" asked Keen.

The young man touched his thumbs to his forefingers and held his right palm facing Keen, with the back of his left hand on his knee, his legs crossed while sitting flat on the ground. "I have been meditating for hours a day since the age of four," he replied. I started with one hour a day and gradually got up to fourteen. I must have a natural ability for this as I've been aware of seeing others' energy fields as long as I can remember."

The young man touched Keen's head briefly. Keen felt a peace that surpasses understanding flood his mind and heart completely. The feeling was enticing. *Would I want to stay in this state forever? There is no sense of excitement here, of adventure, or of a variety of emotions. It's like floating in a giant ocean of relief. I am delighted with this, and yet I miss the love and friendship I feel with Sage.* He became aware of a multitude of worlds and universes, each with their own opulences and activities. *So many forms beyond what Avid and I looked at when I made sculptures! And I have been in so many of them, so many lifetimes.* "What was that?" Keen asked after what seemed like eternity had passed.

The young man laughed slightly. "A person can feel a shadow or a reflection of another's experience sometimes."

"Have you reached the supreme goal?"

"Yes, this is called total contemplation in some schools, and other schools call it *samadhi.* Our practice starts with doing right action and avoiding wrong action. Then we learn how to sit so that the body and mind go into a state of alert relaxation. We then learn how to breathe to put the mind into goodness. As we sit, breathe, and meditate on a chant or mantra—"

"Which mantra?"

"My teacher taught us to chant a Holy Name, one of the infinite names of God, but there are others. After years of meditating with proper sitting posture and breathing, our senses completely leave awareness of the world, something like deep sleep but with inner awareness. At that point we concentrate on the mantra, bringing our mind back to it again and again. At a certain point our concentration becomes effortless like a machine where at first you turn a handle and then it goes on its own power." The young man smiled and closed his eyes for a while. "Then one gets realization that one is a spiritual being separate from body and mind, an observer of likes and dislikes, pleasure and pain. There is difficulty until you get to the point of contemplation or samadhi. It's poison that eventually becomes nectar."

"I read about that—" Keen started to say.

"It's in God's Song and in a lot of other places," one of the introductory students interrupted.

"Yes," the young man continued. "It's in God's Song. Frankly, until contemplation starts going effortlessly, meditation is a lot of work. And, well, I don't know how to say this nicely, but many people don't get to the effortless part for many years, even decades."

"Is samadhi permanent?" the same introductory student asked. The young man looked away for a moment. "That is a question for your teacher. I need to return to my practice." He got up and, taking his mat, wandered into the forest, where he seemed to disappear into the trees.

The introductory students started walking down the mountain back to the campus. The teacher spoke as they walked. "Usually samadhi comes in small glimpses during practice. Again and again we return to the beginning which concerns right and wrong action, and then as we do so, when we meditate again we flow into effortless action easier and samadhi becomes longer and longer. Eventually samadhi comes naturally."

One older women in the introductory group stopped to sit on a rock and everyone else took a break along with her. Keen took the opportunity to sit next to the teacher and ask quietly, "When samadhi becomes the way we are, will we stay still in a meditative trance, or do we become active in a different consciousness, or something else?"

"I'm not sure, Keen, as I know very few people who have come to that stage. Most of those I know stay most of the time in a meditative trance. I know of only two people who claim to have what they call 'walking samadhi' where they maintain their detached, equal vision without any formal meditation at all, though they still do formal meditation at least two hours a day to maintain it."

"Is samadhi static or dynamic?"

"Different people give different answers to that, Keen, but I hope it's dynamic."

As soon as the older woman stood up, they all resumed their walk and returned to the school.

Keen later met Avid and Sage for lunch on the main Mastery Connection campus. As usual, the food was simple to the point of austere while having a stimulating effect on awareness.

Afterward, Avid walked around one of the parks, while Keen and Sage left to sell their art. Avid spent several hours with one man who was struggling with having released the coiled snake energy prematurely. The man said he heard buzzing in his head constantly, could hardly sleep, and had a hard time concentrating. "Playing with mastery in a mechanical way is not for everyone," he told Avid. "Sometimes the teachers are not careful enough about qualifications." He stared long at a bug crawling on a blade of grass. "Meditation is a powerful instrument. Teaching unqualified people is like giving a sharp and large tool to a two-year-old child. And, if you are able to handle it, you can get distracted by the powers."

"My friends and I have met accomplished persons on this path who have powers."

"They are attractive, aren't they?" the man turned his lips into something not quite a smile.

"Ha! Very attractive. My friend, Keen, awakened powers after only a few sessions."

"Really?" the man leaned forward, and he looked intensely at Avid, his eyes alight.

Avid looked over at two birds doing a mating dance in flight. He remembered some reading he hoped to do that evening. He noted the sun's place in the afternoon sky and took what he hoped was an imperceptible deep breath. "Yes, he could go without hunger when fasting, with no fatigue without sleep and he could control his body temperature. They are small powers, but the teachers told him he had such great natural ability that after a year or so he could probably do things that seem like magic. Why do you call them distractions?" Avid looked carefully at the man, who seemed to be much more interested in him now that he had described Keen's small powers than he had been when speaking about his own energy problems. *This man is hungry for power, although he feels such power is not the real goal of his practice. How can someone hunger after what they are convinced is not what they really want?*

The man sat up straight and gave Avid all his attention. "Are you sure that ability was all natural, or was there anything different about his practice? Often people who get something like that so fast know some sort of shortcut not known to others."

Avid looked back at the man. *Ah, we heard about this situation from one of the advanced practitioners. He might well have damaged his subtle energy centers, causing a blockage or the wrong kind of flow. Sounds like he pushes his practice in ways he's not ready for. He thinks he has an intense longing for perfection, but he wants control and powers.* "Sir, I must say, regretfully, that I do not know. You would really need to speak to the teachers who were helping my friend. All I know is that he feels ready to explore the other types of connection schools."

"He is so gifted in Mastery Connection and even thinks to look elsewhere? The fool!" the man almost yelled. He stood and started to walk away. After some paces, he paused, turned and said, "Nice to meet you, young man."

"May you master the mind and body," Avid replied, in the ways of the Mastery Connection.

Knowing Connection Schools
and the Nature Spirits

After finishing the introductory course at the Mastery Connection school they had chosen, Keen, Sage, and Avid went on to explore the Knowing Connection schools. There were certainly many small parks, gardens, and ponds in this area of the city, but the main features of this part of Acumen were undoubtedly the libraries, study halls, discussion halls, and debating arenas. At the entrance to each building and each garden were stone carvings of some sort of guards. Each stone carving had a name chiseled into its base, followed by the word *Yaksha*. "I guess they all have the same family name," Sage joked. Wherever they went people were reading, talking, or writing. Small and large lecture groups and discussion groups were everywhere. Everyone seemed to be carrying books.

Again, they visited the main library and information hub, and again, went through many guidebooks. Unlike the Mastery Connection schools' guidebooks which were mostly about what they *did*, the Knowing Connection schools' guidebooks were mostly about their philosophy and beliefs. It seemed that pretty much all the schools did the same thing — study and discuss philosophy. They all had rules about good and bad actions, which were more or less the same throughout the schools, and similar to the rules at the Mastery Connection schools. What distinguished one Knowing Connection school from another was what philosophy they studied, and who their prominent teachers were. Most of the prominent teachers and philosophers for each school had lived long before — they were only names and stories to today's students. Very few current teachers had personal memories of the main teachers. But the guidebooks also advertised their present teachers, and it seemed that the main "competition" among the schools was between the behavior of the prominent teachers and the details of their philosophy.

All the philosophies had a focus on detachment, realization of the self as the observer, and development of all good qualities. The perfected masters in these schools were described as free from lust, anger, and greed, with equal vision of everyone and everything. All schools emphasized freedom from the body, sense urges, and mundane consciousness.

Keen and Avid found five schools that mentioned "what is both within and without, near and far; what is self-illuminating and filled with love." Sage then narrowed those down to one school. They decided, again, to take the introductory course. Daily for two weeks they met for eight hours with various teachers. Meals were, like in the previous Mastery Connection schools, very simple and austere. If anything, Keen said they were more austere than Mastery Connection, though Avid said he didn't think that was possible. In the Mastery Connection schools, most students and teachers were single celibates, but in the Knowing Connection schools there was an equal mix of ascetics and couples, with and without children.

Three days after beginning the introductory course, Avid was wandering through one of the gardens after lunch. Even after some time of admiring the varieties of flowers and herbs, he noted that he was alone. *Odd that no one else rests here at midday.* He sat leaning against a large, very old tree and closed his eyes. Gradually he felt that someone was staring at him, and he slowly opened his eyes. The man before him looked oddly like the stone carving of guards throughout the area. He had the same slightly rounded stomach, large eyes, protruding ears, and teeth that reminded Avid of fangs. Yet, he also seemed otherworldly. *I wonder if this is, indeed, a man.* Avid thought it appropriate to stand, as the man continued to stare at him. "I — I am Avid, a beginning student here. May I ask who you are?"

"I ask the questions," the man said as a simple statement of fact, not as a challenge. "I guard this garden. It is for the masters only. I keep the treasure here. If you wish to be here, answer my questions."

"I can leave. Please excuse me. I didn't know it was a private area."

"You have come for the treasure. They all do. Why do you seek knowledge of nature?"

"Only with knowledge comes peace. I want relief."

"Why do you want relief?"

"It is natural to want happiness without anxiety. As I have studied the natural world, I have come to believe that."

"We do not give such knowledge easily. But, you have pleased me. I am a Yaksha. Some call us the Huldufolk. Come with me."

Avid found himself carried through a hole he hadn't noticed before at the base of the tree. Although the Yaksha had said "come" Avid didn't feel like he had volition in the matter. They went through the ground but somehow ended up in the sky. Stars and galaxies flew past them. Avid could see the geometry of the cosmos. He had insight into the fundamental nature of reality as if filled with a full understanding. But, a moment later, another, different understanding engulfed him. Theories filled his mind so fast that he could not grab them. One theory contradicted another, yet each seemed to explain everything whenever they first appeared. He was swimming in consecutive moments of surety within an unlimited pool of confusion. Suddenly he was back in the Knowing Connection area, sitting at the feet of a stone Yaksha statue outside the building where his next class was about to start. He stood, and looked at the statue. *Did it smile at me?* He hit his head with his left hand as if to clear his brain, and then went to the class.

Life and death, soul and matter, spiritual equality, insignificance—all such topics were discussed again and again in the classes. After five days, Sage asked Keen for "a talk."

"Sure," he said. *I hope this is not some relationship stuff...*

"Oh, don't worry," Sage laughed as if she read his mind. "But I do want to talk just to you." They walked beneath an archway with stone Yaksha guards, and over to a bench under some trees. A soft wind ruffled the leaves. "All this philosophy has changed me, Keen. I feel a kind of peace and simplicity. I feel compassion without attachment. It's wonderful."

"Wow. I must say I liked the Mastery program better. More of something to do, if we could call it doing at all."

"Yeah, Mastery activity was more just being, rather than doing. But, it does involve the physical more than Knowing, true. What I'm excited about is that Mastery was fixing the mind on one point, but in Knowing I can let my mind explore and wander; I can indulge my curiosity. I love it. I mean, really, I love it. I don't even know if I want to explore the other two kinds of schools. That's what I wanted to talk about. I know we all agreed to try everything—"

"Sage, if you're happy here, I could explore without you. I don't know how Avid feels. I don't feel as satisfied here as I did in Mastery, and yet I didn't feel Mastery is quite what I want. I love the intellectual stimulation here in Knowing. I also feel some detachment, and equilibrium, but not satisfaction. I feel like something is missing."

"Then I'll go with you to explore further. Perhaps there is even something better." Sage took his hand and held it to her cheek. "I love you."

The next day, Avid sat with five others at the feet of one of the greatest Knowing masters. The master sat on a low, flat rock under a tree, and the students sat on shorter wooden seats. Everyone had their own padded mat that they placed on top of their seat. In the immediate area were other groups—some as small as theirs and some as large as fifty—in similar situations. The air was just chilly enough for a light sweater, and the insects buzzing softly reminded Avid of the divine bee-like being. *I would love to see that being again. I have not seen the being since coming to Acumen. Oh — my mind is wandering. Let me listen.* "My dear friends," the master stopped and looked with a smile at each listener. "We want happiness in life, but do we find it? We try to sleep, but the mosquitoes of our enemies' criticisms keep us up at night. We want to delight in family celebrations, but the difficulties involved are like climbing mountains covered with thorns and sharp stones. Poor romantic choices are like windstorms which blind our intelligence. And then there is —"

"The lion of death," one of the students said.

"Yes," the master paused. "Death that makes all worthless, takes away everything and everyone we invested in, and finishes the identity we falsely formed with this body and this world. All the trouble we take is like building a sand castle. So much trouble, and then washed away by the waves." Again, the master paused and then leaned forward. "Our real identity is spiritual. We are temporary travelers in this world only. Realize spirit and there is no more misery, no more desires, no more striving. No more traveling in different bodies."

A small inchworm went carefully from grass to flower at Avid's feet. He watched while continuing to listen, letting the master's words fill his mind and his heart without an inner debate or question. *If I'm going to test this, let me test it completely.* As if someone had walked up from behind quietly and then gradually caught his attention and smiled, Avid found the master's words going beyond something intellectually interesting and satisfying. Detachment filled not only his mind but also his heart. A sense of satisfaction followed. *No use striving for any desires in the world. Just observe.* Floating into his mind came what he'd read in God's Song: "A person in the divine consciousness, although engaged in seeing, hearing, touching, smelling, eating, moving about, sleeping and breathing, always knows within himself that he actually does nothing at all. Because while speaking, evacuating, receiving, or opening or closing his eyes, he always knows that only the material senses are engaged with their objects and that he is aloof from them."

The words came as if brilliant with understanding. He could feel and experience both the futility of ordinary life and himself as the observer, aloof. *This experience is possible by opening oneself to philosophy? Wow. This is not like the changing insights the Yaksha showed me. This is real, like a tree-ripened fresh fruit. Those other insights were like imitation fruit-flavored candies.* But then it faded, like the sun going behind a cloud. The consciousness of being the body, being the doer, of investing hopes and dreams and frustrations in the things of the world returned slowly like a dense cloud. *I can remember that I knew, but now I don't know.* He looked up at the master, a question in his eyes, and realized that the master had finished and was about to stand. *Why did it fade?* Avid also stood, silently, yet something else he had read in God's Song appeared in his awareness as if someone whispered it to him with sharp clarity, "Philosophy brings the truth only after many lifetimes, many births and deaths. Then one finally knows what is within and without." *Lifetimes?*

"Master," Avid said as he quickened his pace to catch up to the master. "How long does it take before the glimpse of truth becomes a constant awareness?"

"It can be a moment, but often it is lifetimes. Remember that the Knowing Connection way is not only study. Most of us take strict vows of living with only the most basic needs for life."

"Those in the Mastery Connection path also do that, don't they?"

"Yes, but there are some differences. They try to stay in a state of contemplation as long as possible, at which times they are unaware of physical needs completely. Of course, they do teach, as we do, that one must do right action and avoid wrong action before meditation—or in our path, wisdom—is even possible. In our path, austerity is a deep and important part, not an adjunct. We are the way of detachment, observing, and denying." The master turned towards a library. "Flow with truth."

"Flow with truth," Avid returned.

As it was not yet lunchtime, Avid decided to sit in the picnic area to wait to meet his friends. He studied a book the great Knowing Connection master had recommended. A woman came and sat near him and asked what he was reading.

"Oh, I read that one too," she said. "In fact, I studied it in depth. Even taught it. I've been in several schools in the Knowing Connection area for ten years."

"You must find this process very satisfying"

She laughed and looked at the clouds for a while before answering. "I achieved perfection, and I didn't like it. I mean, I still believe in a lot of what is taught here, and am keeping some things in my life, but I'm leaving today to go back to the village where I grew up and to help my family with their shop. And, well, to live an ordinary life. My grandfather will be pleased. He practically disowned me when I came here."

Avid was stunned into silence for a bit. "I don't understand. If it's perfection, how it is possible not to like perfection?"

"Detachment and realization that I'm just the observer is such a relief. Pure peace. No suffering. No concerns about anything. Nothing affects you. Nothing. And the peace! Unlimited peace."

"Right."

"Yes, well, I felt connected with everything and everyone as if I was everything and everyone."

"That sounds wonderful."

"Doesn't it?" She leaned back and looked at the clouds again before turning back to Avid. "I found out that I want relationships. Relationships are only possible when we feel we are different individuals from each other. Relationships and compassion are a higher happiness than oneness. At least I want it more. Even if it's all illusion or temporary."

"I… I'm not sure what to say. Should I feel sorry for you, or happy?"

"I'm not sure either!" She smiled without her eyes, and got up to go. Avid saw her meet someone with a round belly and odd teeth as she walked away.

After lunch with Keen and Sage, Avid left to go to where he taught forest craft. He took a route that went through the area close to where the Mastery Connection teachers and students would meditate. The day had warmed, especially in the sun, and Avid decided he had time to stop by a garden near a stream to take a break.

As he found a moss-covered place with the right mix of sun and shade, the water sang and the leaves danced. Birds spoke in their own language about food and enemies. Then, suddenly, all was still. Silence filled the space like a bright light. Avid found himself not wanting to move and hardly aware of his breathing. Soon the divine being, the bee guide, shimmered and shone near him, and Avid felt something he could only describe as compassion fill him. The silence continued both forever and only for a moment — impossible to tell as time seemed everywhere and nowhere.

Without effort or strain, Avid looked at the being and thought, *I seek who is far away but always very near, within everything and yet outside of everything, walking yet not walking. The energetic source of all knowledge, happiness, and existence. I seek the essence.*

"How will you know you have found the essence?" the being seemed to have an audible voice, unlike Avid's silent thought communication, but even the audible voice felt as if it were heard by the mind rather than the ear. "If you don't understand the signs of achieving the goal, you will not know you are getting closer."

Avid felt a quiet alertness and he left his mind and heart open. *The indications are there in what we studied. In the Song, God's Song. Equilibrium, and experience of being an observer, separate from body and mind. Boundless happiness. I have felt a bit of these so far here in Acumen, at the schools. And with you.* Avid felt as if his thoughts were smiling.

"And love?"

In the stillness, Avid felt something stir within him. He could say he loved his parents, his departed grandmother, and his brothers and sisters. He loved his friends, especially Keen and Sage. He had loved animals such as horses, cows, sheep, and goats. He had loved the natural world. Although romantic love did not interest him, his life seemed full of what is called love. *I already have love.*

"The essence is filled with a deeper and different love. It's like an ever-flowing stream of life-giving nectar. When the plug of pride and ego is taken from the inner core, that nectar of love flows into a person of its own accord. Love means that the beloved's happiness is your own happiness and you seek no separate happiness, because the happiness of love fills you completely. Find the one who is the highest ideal of love, whose name is like perfume poured out. Find the one whose eyes are like the eyes of doves, or deer, or petals of a lotus flower. Find the all-attractive one."

As before in their meetings, the being faded and the sounds and movements of the world returned. Avid's awareness was quickly drawn to beautiful flowers filled with bees where the being had been. Some of the bees were especially covered in pollen, and swollen with honey. *Does my friend — is this a friend, or a guide or both — really have the form of a bee in this world?* The thought again made Avid feel like his thoughts were smiling. He started to walk towards where his students would soon be waiting for him. *My feelings and experiences, understandings, and happiness so far in the Mastery Connection and Knowing Connection schools — could they be called love? If they are love, who is the beloved object of that love? Or are they teaching liberation from illusion without love? Whom do I love? And what, really does it mean to love?* As Avid came into the area where the city meets the forest, he saw a small group of students either already waiting for him or walking towards the waiting place, eager to learn forest craft. All other thoughts quickly went from his mind.

When Avid met with Keen and Sage the next morning, he told them, "When we finish our introductory course here in two days, I would like to go to the Devotion Connection schools next.

We planned to stay a month to check things out, and it's already been five weeks."

Keen looked up from fixing his shoes. "Ok with me, and I do want to check out the Action Connection schools also, to take the introductory courses from the best in each group."

"Sure," Avid replied. "Ok with you, Sage?"

"Yes," she replied. "That will mean staying in Acumen at least four weeks more just to decide where to study further. I must say that I have found such peace and detachment here in this Knowing Connection school that I am satisfied without looking any more. But I will stick with you two until we make up our minds."

"And, suppose each find what we look for in different places than the others?" Keen asked, looking at his wife with intense curiosity.

"Don't be concerned about tomorrow, for tomorrow will be concerned for itself. A day's own trouble is sufficient for it," she quoted.

"Don't be concerned with gain and safety but be established in the self," Keen responded with another quote.

"Touché!" Avid said, and they all laughed.

Devotion Connection Schools and the Elephant in Musth

The eastern section of Acumen was quite different from the western and northern sections. Here it was not clear to Avid, Keen, and Sage if they were seeing schools or places of worship. Many of the schools looked like gatherings for prayer, or song and dance, as they had heard from Gurvi when they first arrived. While the Mastery and Knowing areas — especially Mastery — were mostly full of natural, though perhaps stark, beauty, this section was filled with architecture as gorgeous and inviting as the best nature has to offer. Buildings were especially tall or expansive or both. Intricate carvings and designs were everywhere, as were various symbols of ancient and modern teachers. Some places had decorations only of symbols and designs, while others had detailed sculptures or paintings of enlightened teachers, showing the stories of their lives. There was art of God as creator of the world along with demigods and angels. The most amazing art, Avid remarked, was of God in heaven, the spiritual world. Some of this art showed scenes far beyond anything imagined in this world, and some was so colorful, so detailed, that the three often forgot where they were and got lost in the visions.

Gardens of fragrant flowers filled with bees and birds, and ponds filled with shining, colored fish surrounded the buildings. Sculptures of symbols, teachers, God, and heavenly beings were enshrined in various places in these gardens. Often a small protective and decorative structure surrounded the sculptures. Two or three areas they passed, however, looked like a storm had ravaged everything. Trees were broken, sculptures shattered, and the ground vegetation randomly torn up. Surprisingly, the devastation would seem to create a kind of path, next to which everything was untouched, as if something or someone had rushed through with such force and speed that destruction ensued as a side effect. Along with gardens and places of worship there were also libraries and classrooms everywhere.

As they walked through the schools and gardens to the main library and welcome area, the sounds of heavenly music came from various directions. Some were choirs of only human voices that seemed to soar beyond the possibilities of voice. Some were group or individual singing with intricate accompaniment of various instruments. Some were call-and-response singing. Some were more appropriately called chants rather than songs, which reminded Keen of the meditative mantras in the Mastery Connection school. In some cases, bells, gongs or singing bowls dominated, and in others the variety of instruments sounded like a symphony. Some music seemed as ancient as eternity, and some was of a more modern mood. Avid pointed out several times where they could see through windows or doors dozens or even hundreds of people not only singing but also dancing. Dancing in some places was highly stylized with colorful garments and synchronized groups. In other places people were dancing with such joy and abandon that no particular pattern was discernible and, Sage noted, there was no chance such dancing was rehearsed. In a few places, groups of singers and dancers sat in gardens or even danced in a walking style on the paths. Flavors of music from all the cultures and traditions of the world floated through the air, with new ones getting louder as others grew softer with each block or turn of corner. Somehow the various types of music harmonized with each other, while remaining distinct.

It seemed to Sage that there were more schools here than in the other two areas they had explored, and the chief librarian at the Devotion Connection central library and welcome center confirmed her guess. "But there are also many Action Connection schools," the librarian added. "Not very many people can take up the paths of Mastery or Knowing. Those paths are not really suited for most people to follow long-term. Their introductory courses, especially in Mastery, often are overflowing, however." The librarian leaned forward, glanced around, and spoke so as to be barely audible. "Everyone feels the path they have chosen is the best. In many ways, there is more competition among the various schools of the same type of connection than between the schools from different connection areas! There are a few people who see the benefits of each connection way, and each school. But to be unbiased —" The librarian relaxed and leaned into the back of the chair, "the Devotion Connection schools — at least the best ones — have the best features of all the other connection paths. In the top schools here, they meditate, they study philosophy, they do enlightened action, and they live lives of joy and song."

"Certainly, a lot of song!" Keen remarked, and they all laughed quietly.

"Sing the Sacred Sounds!" the librarian responded enthusiastically. It would take a few days before the friends realized they had just heard the typical Devotion Connection salutation.

Again, the three went through guidebooks and brochures, with the help of the chief librarian and other guides there. Some schools emphasized heavenly rewards here "similar to Dutiful," pointed out a guide. Others focused more on heaven after death. Some described both heaven here and after death. Others presented the goal as freedom from suffering and human faults. A few schools mixed those with descriptions of love, and some very few stated that the only goal is loving service to the Divine, all life, and all matter. Even those latter schools' brochures added that heaven here and now, heaven after death, and freedom from pain and faults would be side effects.

Avid picked out four schools that promoted loving service with everything else as side effects — including mastery over the body and mind as well as knowledge. "If Devotion Connection has the best aspects from the other paths, why have the other paths at all?" he mused.

Sage looked at him for a while until he shifted his eyes. "Maybe some people like things to be simple," she said, trying not to sound defensive.

"It's not just that everything is included, Sage," Avid said carefully. "It's also the description in these of the Divine. Look! Here God is described as—"

"—what is both within and without, near and far, what is self-illuminating and filled with love," Sage said from memory, but with feeling.

"Well, yes, yes, and more. Look. Not just that, but also all-attractive. And as full of sweetness, a herder of animals in a pasture in a place filled with an infinite variety of loving beings. We read about such an understanding in the books back home, the book you talked about with Gurvi."

"Oh," Keen said, "this one describes God as a shepherd. Is that what you mean? Isn't that just poetry?"

"Maybe," Avid read through several again. "Here, in this one it says God is herding cows, buffalo, and goats. And it doesn't seem to be some poetic idea, but a description of an ultimate reality."

"A heaven?" Keen asked.

"Something like that. There's a detailed description. The idea is that God as the King of Kings is incomplete. Even powerful people on this planet like to spend time in a country atmosphere away from all the awe and reverence. A complete picture of the Soul of All is the Divine in simplicity, as if he is a herder of animals. Those who love the essence in this mood eschew grandeur in favor of intimacy and sweetness."

Keen picked one school out of Avid's four choices and they all signed up for the introductory course. The librarian had been correct that elements from all three of the others—Mastery, Knowing, and Action—were included in the Devotion

Connection, though it was a mood and life of love, affection, and service that was emphasized. Mastery of the mind and senses was not done through mechanically shifting the body, breath, and concentration, but through devotion to the all-attractive ideal and the resulting reciprocation of grace. Philosophy in this school made you detached, Sage noted, not through logic but through increasing an interest in the all-attractive being, which, again, attracts grace. And action was not just enlightened duty (as they heard would be found in the Action Connection schools) but service to the all-attractive being, which yet again, attracts grace. "They should call this school 'Grace Connection,' though it is devotion which inspires grace," she said with perhaps an edge of criticism.

That evening Avid got a message from his father. While Sage heard from someone in her family a few times a week, and Keen maybe once a week, this was only the second time since they left their home that Avid had heard from any of his family members. Out of everyone, he'd felt closest to Grandma and Mohah until the day he left for Acumen. But Grandma was gone, and Mohah had cut him off. *I don't get in touch with them much myself either, so I can't complain.* The message was short and to the point: Pena had found a job she really liked, and Tavis thought she might be in love with someone suitable this time. *I suppose they'll want me to go home for a wedding. At least Pena is doing better. I hope she's learned her lesson.*

Keen said he loved the concept of a reality where there are endless life forms, and where the Divine has an infinite variety of personal relationships with all of them. So, he had picked the school where God was described as a herder of cows, buffalo, and goats (and perhaps sheep also, he had added with a soft laugh). He was filled with enthusiasm about meditating on these descriptions through his sculptures. Avid pointed out that these descriptions were not exactly of worldly animals but of saints in a spiritual heaven. Saints in the form of goats! The idea amused and intrigued Avid, and made Keen ponder how to translate such into clay, if it were possible at all. The guidebook explained to potential skeptics that all the forms of this world have their counterparts in an original world of spirit, and that each form there is a particular soul's expression to exchange love with the Divine in a particular way. The explanation reminded Sage of one philosopher who suggested that whatever we experience in this world is the shadow of its archetype in reality.

Although they went to the introductory course at the same school, each subsequently chose different groups and teachers within that school. From the first five minutes, Avid felt that he was with like-minded people and had come home, which, though a cliché, seemed to best describe what he was feeling. *I remember talking to Grandma in what I now understand was the Forest of Material Enjoyment about where our home was. When we finally got a house in the city, my mother and Sarala often said how glad and relieved they were to have a home. But I never really felt that way. I kept feeling like a nomad and a guest. Why would I now feel at home in a school? But I do!*

The days started with group singing and dancing, and then individual contemplation. Like in the Mastery School, the meditation was on a prayer, chant, or mantra, along with inner thought on the descriptions they studied in their classes. Keen found this meditation somewhat more challenging than that of the Mastery Connection, but after two days he discovered that if he used what he had learned there, his mind easily stayed fixed. Overall, he found the experience much more profound, though it took him a while before the reason became apparent — this meditation matured into a custom fit for his innermost nature. Avid memorized this method: "The mantra or prayer is the bow, the pure living being is the arrow, and the target is the Supreme Being." Sage loved the classes after meditation, where they studied philosophy and logic, along with stories of saints and God.

Avid found himself drawn into the stories such that he almost felt part of them. While aware that his mother and Mohah would scoff at the fantastic descriptions, he had personal experiences in his own life which resisted ordinary explanation — his memories sparked by Keen's sculptures, and of course, his mysterious bee-like guide. Even experts in Mastery Connection schools could seemingly do the impossible. Why not, then, be open to a wider view of reality than ordinary life?

And the singing was no different! Many of the songs opened doors in his awareness, letting out long-hidden colorful birds of expression of which he had up to that point been only dimly aware. When a teacher mentioned that a group was going to visit the Sacred Garden, the most important holy place, later in the year, Avid was entranced, feeling as if an inner urge was calling him to say *yes* without knowing anything more. He made an appointment with that teacher to learn more.

That afternoon, Avid and Keen took a long walk to where the fields met the forest while Sage worked on a new tapestry. There they encountered elephants harvesting teak. "The elephants respect the forest. They are much better than people using tools to clear cut," Keen said. "They only pick the right trees, and, because they can go through all sorts of terrain, no one needs to build roads." A male elephant with huge tusks picked up a log and put it on a pile, while a female elephant with shorter tusks pushed the logs. The mahouts spoke gently to the huge creatures, who affectionately embraced their masters with their trunks. "Useful, gentle, and intelligent friends," Keen said as he stroked an elephant whose mahout guided her near him.

Suddenly loud trumpeting broke the air. Small explosions of trees crashing spooked everyone, who moved out of the paths and into the forest. Another strange sound also vibrated in the forest. A large bull elephant emerged, with temporin liquid oozing down the side of his head, and urine covering the insides of his thighs. Looking in all directions, he trumpeted and challenged and then charged towards where the forest met cultivated land. "Musth," Keen whispered. "The maddened elephant is in musth."

As the trumpeting got quieter, gradually the elephant keepers, along with Keen and Avid, emerged from the forest with their animals. "A wild one?" a younger mahout asked of a grey-haired, muscular man.

The older man shook his head and sighed. "No, I know the mahout for that one. Careless fool! One must know the signs, and cut down food and water to the bull before it gets dangerous. Then everything passes safely after a few days. Otherwise the animal is dangerous for many months."

The young man shrugged his shoulders, "Well, at least my brother will have work repairing the gardens this one destroys on its rampaging path. Hope the bull doesn't kill or hurt anyone."

"We will have to lure him back into the deep forest, where he can stay until it's over. But it's dangerous, very dangerous. That bull can kill those he dearly loved just yesterday. A bull in musth destroys anything and anyone and is easily irritated. He thinks he is king of the world."

Keen and Avid quickly left back to Acumen. On the way, they saw a freshly destroyed garden, and, in the distance, the bull entering the deep forest.

Later that day, Avid made sure he was early for his appointment with Ucitel, the teacher who had spoken about visiting a sacred place. "Oh, you're one of the introductory students!" the teacher said, rising from his chair with a smile as Avid entered.

"Yes, and I love it here. I love the descriptions of the Divine, the Supreme Friend, and his world, the explanations of the science of life, the singing, the meals, the services we all do — everything. I would like to visit a holy place. What did you call it?"

"A crossing place, which translates as *teertha* in the ancient tongue, the language of the celestials and angels. Teerthas are like portals that can take you to a spiritual realm if you know how to respect them. They also have some effect even if you don't know." He thought for a while and then said, "Actually, the Sacred Garden is more than a teertha. It's the chief kind of sacred space, called a dhahm." They had both sat down by now, but Ucitel continued to smile. "A dhahm is, itself, a spiritual realm, not just a portal to one. Here, take this information on our journey. You can start with us from here, or you can join at any point on the way. We'll be leaving soon." He handed Avid some colorful documents and a small booklet. "The full name of the place is 'Garden of Sacred Fragrance.'"

"Long name."

"Yes, so we usually just call it the Sacred Garden. The Supreme Friend can be found there playing as if a simple cowherd."

"What is the result of your practice of Devotion Connection?" Avid asked, while carefully holding the papers and book in his lap.

"Well, in one sense it's a very private thing," Ucitel paused for several minutes and looked at a painting on the wall, his eyes even brighter and wider, but now seeming no longer to smile. Avid followed the teacher's gaze and noticed the painting depicted the cowherd dancing. He wondered if the teacher saw merely a painting, or was gazing as if through a window to another realm.

Ucitel finally continued, "I was speaking to a senior student from one of the most revered Mastery Connection schools the other day. She described how she feels like an observer of this world and of her body and mind, and how her desires to enjoy this world have diminished. I realized that I experience all that she experiences, but almost without noticing it. It's as if what they are aiming for as the main goal are merely side effects of devotional love."

"What is the main effect of devotional love?" asked Avid.

"Ha! Do you really want to know?"

"Indeed."

"It's described in the books, like God's Song. What more do you need than that?" He leaned back and smiled again slightly, mostly with his eyes. "Come to the Sacred Garden with us. Take the journey. There are signposts along the way. You will find not just the essence of life and the universe, but the nectar of love of God. You will also find yourself. Any gifts available in this world are nothing in comparison."

"Quite a promise," Avid smiled.

"Indeed."

Avid decided that Ucitel was not going to reveal anything more of his inner personal life to an introductory student and left for the main meal.

The meals at the Devotion Connection school they had chosen were extraordinary. The preparations were fresh and from seasonal produce. Unlike the spartan food in the Mastery and Knowing Connection schools, meals here were of great variety and taste. In fact, the tastes were astonishing. The effects of eating produced the clarity and energy they had felt from food in the other schools, and then included a feeling that the heart was expanding with compassion and affection. A section of the curriculum was dedicated to preparation and serving of food with devotion, and buildings were set aside for "spiritual culinary science."

That evening Avid looked up in God's Song the signs of perfection in devotion. He read:

> He who does not hate illumination, attachment and delusion when they are present or long for them when they disappear; who is unwavering and undisturbed through all these reactions of the material qualities, remaining neutral and transcendental, knowing that matter alone is active; who is situated in the self and regards alike happiness and distress; who looks upon a lump of soil, a stone and a piece of gold with an equal eye; who is equal toward the desirable and the undesirable; who is steady, situated equally well in praise and blame, honor and dishonor; who treats alike both friend and enemy.

Avid closed the book. *That's the same kind of result those in the Mastery and Knowing Connection schools aim for. But that teacher today, here, said these effects are just automatic, and the main effect is beyond.* He opened the book again, this time to another section, and read:

> This perfection is characterized by one's ability to see the self via the pure mind and to relish and rejoice in the self. In

that joyous state, one is situated in boundless transcendental happiness, realized through transcendental senses. Established thus, one never departs from the truth, and upon gaining this one thinks there is no greater gain. Being situated in such a position, one is never shaken, even in the midst of the greatest difficulty. This indeed is actual freedom from all miseries arising from material contact.

Again, Avid closed the book, and this time he put it on the table. *The teacher said we would see our real self, and here in God's Song it says we will relish and rejoice in the self. The other schools teach something similar, but when it comes to describing the nature of the self, this Devotion school gives so much detail. To love our real self, to know our real self, even to rejoice in our real self. I wonder what that would really mean?* Avid noticed how dark it was outside his window and started getting ready for bed. *I've been reading and thinking for a long time!* As he got into his bed, and started to fall asleep, suddenly he found himself fully alert but relaxed, almost in the same state as when he would interact with his divine bee-like guide. Understanding filled him like a light gradually increasing in brightness. *My real self is filled with love! I have a particular kind of love for the Supreme, and for everyone! A pure love! And, it's a flavor and type of love that only I have, and I love that flavor and relationship more than anything, anywhere, ever! Oh!* The feeling faded like a light gradually getting dimmer, but it took over an hour before he fell into a deep and peaceful sleep.

In the evening after the fifth day, Sage prepared a meal for the three of them as she had learned in the Devotion Connection school. "I do think my desire for philosophy is satisfied here," she said. "Well, mostly. I could easily enroll in this school as a regular student, but I would want to visit that Knowing Connection school also for some classes."

"Ok with me. Do you want to try the Action Connection schools before making a final decision?" Keen directed his question at Sage.

Yet, it was Avid who answered. "I feel more satisfied here than I have felt anywhere else before in my life. I'm happy to check out Action Connection but, as we skipped the city of Dutiful, I doubt I'll be interested."

Sage nodded in agreement.

The next day as the three walked together, Keen started talking to a man who had followed the program for a Devotion Connection school similar to the one they were attending, but had left and become discouraged. "I practiced everything for ten years," the former student said, "but my bad habits came back, and I don't feel that I ever found the nectar, or the essence I was seeking. I feel like I'm trying to find fruit after a storm has devastated the garden. My teachers and the senior students said my problems came from ego—"

"—in all the schools, they blame ego for any problems with following their method, don't they?" Avid responded.

"Ha! Yes. Here it was more specific, that my problems with making progress came from not treating others well and offending them. But, I'm confident that was not my problem." He spoke the word *confident* with finality. "Actually, the more I applied myself, the more people respected me and treated me like a saint. Maybe those who felt offended were particularly sensitive." A smirk moved his lips with contempt. "It's not criticism when we speak honestly about other's problems in order to have ethical standards."

"So, what do you think was the cause?" asked Keen.

"I'm not sure there is any way to find the essence of life, at least not any way you can count on. There doesn't seem to be a formula. You tend your garden and a random storm destroys it," said the man.

Avid looked at the mountains. *It is not a storm. The mountains keep out the storms. It's an elephant in musth.* He turned his attention back to the conversation.

"I thought the whole point of the Devotion and Knowing Connection schools is to give up on formulaic ideas; the formulaic ideas are mostly in Dutiful, in the Mastery Connection, and the Action Connection schools. At least that's what I've heard," said Keen.

"If there is no formula, then how can there be a school, and a path to follow? It doesn't make sense to me anymore," the man shook his head.

Keen remembered the talk he had heard the other day. *The teacher said that one of the best ways to show devotion to God is to deal with other beings and things so as to make God smile.* He replied, "Sometimes the path of devotion is said to be the easiest since loving others is natural, and we just have to turn that love to the Supreme. But, on the other hand, it can be said to be the hardest because love is not a formula. It's a personal relationship, and a mysterious one."

"Thanks, but I think I'm done with mysterious paths. I just want the solid ground of life. I might move back to Dutiful. Things are simple there," the man said with some force.

"Do they even speak in Dutiful about finding the nectar essence of life?" Sage asked.

"No, not much." The man paused for a long time. "Not much. But maybe that's what I want right now, to forget."

Keen smiled and nodded as the man picked up a large bag, turned, and walked towards the center of town. Avid and Sage shook their heads slightly.

That evening, as Keen worked in his studio, he sat and held the sculpture of an emerging butterfly he had created on the day he had dedicated himself to nectar seeking. He considered how what he learned and experienced in the various schools since then seemed to flow from his hands into the clay. His focus had always been on realistic depictions of the things of the world, and now he also tried to convey more esoteric subjects. His technique to do so involved how he portrayed the expressions and movements of individual figures, as well as the relationship of the figures to each other. More and more, he felt a connection to the essence of existence while absorbed in the process of molding the clay. But, when looking at the finished products, his awareness could easily shift to focus only on the technical aspects — how he had plied his art. Increasingly, though, people who came to see or buy often remarked how his work transported them to epiphanies. It became almost effortless for him to sell enough — especially when combined with the sales of his wife's textile art — to live comfortably and donate generously. He wondered whether what they would learn in the remaining quadrant of the city could possibly add any dimension to his work.

Action Connection Schools and the Giant Hornets

Keen's first remark when they went to the south of Acumen was that the Action Connection schools seemed almost like a city within the city, as Gurvi had predicted. The setup of the schools was quite different from the other quadrants. Although some schools taught the general theory and practice of Action Connection, most taught the system within a specialized area. For example, there was a school about government, another about farming, one about weaving, and others about any occupation one could think of. There were also schools about family relationships and schools about living as a renounced, detached person. Some schools included courses about how to manage extreme old age and death, and others had courses about how to study better as a student.

There was no overarching feel or plan to the area as each type of school had a radically different atmosphere, buildings, and so forth. For example, in the schools for farming and gardening, there were fields, gardens, and animals such as sheep, goats and cows. But in the schools for governance and leadership there were extensive libraries and assembly halls as well as martial arts practice arenas. Like in the other three city quadrants, there was an overall information center and master library with many helpful guides and librarians. As they opened the library door, a huge hornet, almost as big as Sage's little finger, flew into the library with them. "That's a young queen," Keen remarked.

A librarian sat down with the three of them at a round table with racks in the center filled with books and brochures. She seemed younger than Sage in physical appearance, but when she explained — because they asked — about her education and life experience, it was obvious that she was a few years older.

"Have you lived in Dutiful?" she asked after they exchanged pleasantries.

"No, we just went through it on our way here," the three practically said in unison. The librarian laughed.

"Well, see, in most cities, towns and villages, people don't even do action properly, and it's hard to learn Action Connection without first knowing how to act."

"But, in Dutiful —" Sage started but then thought better of it and closed her mouth quickly.

The librarian looked quickly at each of them and then leaned forward a bit. "When those in Dutiful get free of the enchantments of the two witches there, they may come here for the next step. Here we equally honor all the paths from there. Among the main good things in Dutiful is a clear understanding of duty and responsibility. Good action."

"Is knowing what is good action really so difficult?" asked Sage.

A group of people in protective clothing interrupted their discussion as they headed for a corner of the library. "Is there a hornet nest in here?" asked Keen.

"Generally, they don't get in, but yes they are very dangerous."

Avid remembered discussions he and Keen had long ago about Keen's clay figures, "Aren't honeybees and hornets mortal enemies?" he asked.

"Indeed, they are," answered Keen. He then turned to the librarian, "About good action, well, we three all have professions and we grew up in families. Is there more to know?" he asked, trying hard not to sound as if he thought the topic ludicrous.

"In a sense, yes," the librarian answered, trying to ignore the group taking a sealed box with the hornet nest outside. "What I usually suggest for those who skipped Dutiful is to try the schools in the other parts of Acumen. But, sometimes our schools will work for you, too. If you would like the introductory course—"

Again, in unison, the three said, "Yes," and then they all laughed.

"Ok, then. Best to first go to one of the schools about general practice and theory. Most of those have a five-day introduction. For those who skipped Dutiful, the full course in one of those schools is usually one year." She paused, knowing the effect her words have on most people. "Yes, well. After that time, you would go to a specialized school for your particular craft. You would also attend a specialized school for your time of life and way of living—you two are married, yes?" She looked from Keen to Sage.

Keen nodded and Sage blushed slightly.

"And you?" she looked at Avid. "Are you married, or do you plan to marry?"

"No," Avid said. "I have never had an interest or desire. I want to... I can't really explain what I want to do."

"Perfect, yes, we have a school for you after you would finish the theory course. Here," she handed Avid a small booklet with a cover like a dancing fire. "This explains about the schools that teach how to live like an ascetic. Even if you don't stay in our part of Acumen, the information here should help you in whatever path you take."

Avid carefully opened the book. Looking at the table of contents, he saw a section about the schools in the Action Connection section which taught ascetic living. Then there were sections from something called An Ancient History of the One Full of All Glories. In the old tongue it was called the Bhagavat Purana. *Oh, we read parts of this book. It has many volumes.* "What do I owe you for this?" he asked the librarian with happiness.

"Just put some offering in the box on your way out," she said. "Whatever you like. And this is the main season when those hornets protect their nests. Be careful."

Sage decided to spend the rest of her morning in the library on her own. She got a stack of books on creating textile art as an Action Connection practice, and was looking through them, when a woman around her age sat at the same table. "I haven't seen you here before," that woman said quietly. "Oh, we just came to this section. We haven't been long in Acumen altogether," Sage replied just above a whisper. "I've been here two years. I love the idea of worship through work. It seems so elegant and natural," she looked at Sage's books. "I guess you're an artist."

"Yes."

"Well, I should probably warn you," the girl looked around and sighed. "Action Connection is really hard. You know, in normal life, or even what they do in Dutiful, you work for some purpose, and then you enjoy what you worked for. Working that way is sort of what we do automatically. What the animals do."

"Right. But in Action Connection you give up the results of work, yes?"

"Exactly. It seems natural because we're doing what we would do anyway, but with a different mood." She paused again. "But, it's very difficult. Without enjoying the results of work, it's a struggle to be motivated. Life seems so abstract. Just working for purification and freedom. I often feel like I'm trying to drink from an empty glass."

"Doesn't detached work lead to peace and a greater satisfaction? We studied that."

"Eventually, logically it should, yes. While getting there it's so... so... frustrating. And the most difficult thing —," her voice dropped even more to a whisper, "is that it's hard to feel detached from the labels we need in order to know what work to do. We need to work according to a label without identifying with the label."

Just then, three giant hornets buzzed around them.

"We need to get out of here," the girl said, and they both quickly left.

That afternoon, Avid, Keen, and Sage started in the introductory course on theory. They sat in the shade of ripening fruit trees. The first main point seemed to be doing various jobs according to individual nature, and according to rules of what is and is not proper behavior. Most of the rules seemed like obvious basic moral and ethical principles, though Keen mentioned after class that in their home city not everyone aimed for such high standards. That first point about working according to one's nature, the teacher explained, is exactly what is done in the city of Dutiful. The next point, about working according to principles, involved what connected the practitioner of Action Connection to the essence. As the teacher was speaking, one student swatted and killed a giant hornet without anyone else noticing. As the hornet was dying, it released pheromones which alerted the nearby hive of nearly 700 members. Unlike bees which hesitate to sting as doing so means their death, hornets can sting again and again with terrible venom.

Before the teacher could describe the principles of Action Connection, the hive started to swarm. Keen, who had studied hornets long ago, knew the hierarchical cruelty these poisonous creatures practiced among their own kind. Power struggles between males and females, with violent mating, induced queens to try to escape and remain barren. Lesser members of the nest would starve if food was scarce. While they appeared to function as a harmonious whole in their colony, class and gender struggle permeated giant hornet society. Now, however, with a common enemy, they temporarily united.

Seasoned practitioners in Action Connection regularly drilled in dealing with hornets, but these introductory students were mostly unprepared. The teacher tried to stem the panic and prevent stings. People sometimes died if they were stung too many times. Keen, also skilled, directed his wife and friend and they ducked into a nearby building unscathed. But the next day, when the class met again, some students were still nursing swollen fingers or feet. About a third of those who had been present during the swarm were not in class again at all.

One young woman whose left side was dotted with swollen bumps asked the teacher, "Action Connection starts with deciding on our work according to our type and interest. In Dutiful, different types would exploit others. Can that happen here too?" "Exploitation based on how we label our type does, indeed, poison connection, yes. Safety is in the principles," the teacher replied. "The principles are best applied as a whole society."

Avid remembered one of Keen's sculptures. *One hornet enters a hive, and the bees combine to form a ball around it. The hornet is surrounded and heated until it dies and cannot bring the rest of its nest to destroy the hive.*

Avid wrote down the principles as follows: 1 be attentive to the work itself each moment instead of focusing on a final result, 2 share the results of work as in giving charity, 3 protect the sources of wealth, rather than exploiting them, 4 work without an egotistical sense of being the doer or being one's label, 5 compete only with those of the same vocation, 6 have cooperation and equality with those of other vocations, 7 allow the flow of each labeled type to correct and adjust the others, and 8 offer the work itself, along with the results of work, as a sacrifice to the Universe and the Soul of the Universe. Avid felt that last point had a strong overlap with Devotion Connection.

After the five days, they each visited schools that related to their particular area of work and life situation. Avid was pleasantly surprised to find a school for finding connection with the essence through forest craft. *If I need to do this to maintain myself anyway, it would be nice to learn how to do it in a "connection way."* The forest crafts area was at the edge of the actual forest, and included classrooms with buildings. Avid was surprised to see that most of what he knew (and taught!) and much more was being taught here, but with a different flavor than he already knew. Avid went to one of the teachers during a break. "Could I take a course here even if I did not take the full overall theory course, and I skipped Dutiful?" he asked with little hope.

"We get asked that now and then," the teacher considered.

"You can come for the short, two-week course if you like. It's not a beginners' level — we figure you already know a lot."

"Well, I do know a lot of forest craft," Avid replied.

"Ok, we can see you in two days, then. Worship through work!"

"Worship through work!" Avid responded.

Commitment comes in stages with some obvious times of choice. The choice to study essence seeking while in their home city, what to speak of the choice to leave their home for Acumen, each marked dedication to something beyond ordinary life. Yet, they were still explorers, like shoppers holding merchandise and turning it over in their hands, weighing the value against the price. Only with the next level of dedication could a serious quest begin.

The Dedication

Avid, Keen, and Sage all decided to commit themselves to a Devotion Connection school and to make that path the central point in their lives. Sage also enrolled in some classes in a Knowing Connection school, and Keen arranged for a Mastery Connection teacher to give him weekly guidance. After several months in Acumen, Keen and Sage had gotten their own house, an easy walk from their studio and the programs they attended at the Devotion Connection school. Avid figured he had enough money to take a break from working for two weeks and attend the forest craft program at the Action Connection school. At the very least, he reasoned, doing so would make him a better teacher.

Avid loved the help he got at the Action Connection forest craft program. He discovered, though, that what he was gaining in devotion helped him more in action than the other way around. It was as if growing in devotion helped him to understand how to do the same work he had always done, but in an entirely different mood and awareness. He was bringing his meditative state into his work. For example, one day his planned class was on distinguishing edible from poisonous wild fruits. Formerly, he would have felt the planning, setting up, and teaching to be hard work aimed at the pleasure of having students properly identify the fruits, and then prepare a simple meal. Now, he offered each step of his teaching process before and during the class to the Supreme Friend and let go of any conception of success or failure. His sense of owning, doing, or controlling receded to the background. Joy arose moment by moment as his effort and the work itself all were saturated with wisdom and detachment. The happiness was in the moments rather than the results. Avid felt he no longer identified as someone expert in forest craft, or as the son of Tavis and Dųma, or as anything in this world. Those were only roles that he played, while secretly having a very different identity. He sang: "This world has become full of wonderful meaning, there is no more fear, and I am immersed in the ocean of pure joy."

Commitment to a school meant eventually choosing a main teacher who would give personal guidance for one's practice. While the three friends each dedicated themselves to the same Devotion Connection school where they had taken the introductory course, each chose a different main teacher after several months of carefully observing the teacher's behavior and asking thoughtful questions. At Avid's ceremony of dedication to his main teacher, he felt he stepped through a doorway into another phase of his life. His main teacher then instructed him in a daily practice of song, study, and meditation on holy names of the Supreme Friend, in his mood of a simple cowherd. Avid found much joy in doing simple, even menial, service for his teacher out of gratitude. While all the help and instructions he received were valuable, Avid particularly appreciated this one, which his teacher repeated often: "Love all beings and all things. Serve all and never exploit. Especially love the nectar seekers, whoever they may be and wherever they are. Love the sacred sounds and prayer. Love the teachers. Love sacred places. Love the path of love itself, which is surrender of all that is false and acceptance of devotion to all that is true. Have peace, forgiveness, and most of all, courage to conquer fear."

"My dear Avid," his main teacher had told him, "If you follow these instructions, the path to the essence of life and the unlimited nectar of happiness will always be shown to you. It will be revealed. You will know what ought to be done and what ought not to be done, what is to be feared and what is not to be feared, what is binding and what is liberating." Avid yearned to have those words truly describe him, and wondered what it would mean to achieve that state of being.

PART FOUR

Avid's Journey

Home

One day, nearly a year after they had all left their home city, the three met for dinner, and Keen and Sage announced to Avid that they were expecting a child. After heartily congratulating them, Avid had his own announcement to make. "I'm going with one of the teachers from our school to visit the Sacred Garden. We're leaving in a few days. I'm not going with them from the start because Pena is getting married and my father really wants me to come home for the wedding. I... I want to go also. I'm happy that Pena is getting settled in life. So, I'm going to travel alone to the wedding, and then from there I hope to meet up with the group. By the time I get back, your child might be walking. Or even talking."

Avid packed very lightly. He planned to walk or take public vehicles. Maybe sometimes people would offer him a ride. He did not plan where he would stay. Such was the practice of an ascetic he had learned from the book he had received in the Action Connection library. He packed that book and God's Song, clothes for warm or cold weather, a blanket, food such as dried fruits that would last long on a journey, and some personal essentials. He was determined to only pack what he could easily carry without the help of animal or vehicle, or even simple wheels.

With great care Avid took from the top of a shelf what would have looked like a framed picture to a casual observer. It had been resting upon a beautifully embroidered lace mat Grandma purchased years ago in exchange for semi-precious gems they had found in the forest. The frame was hand-carved out of a rare and shiny wood Mohah found deep in the forest when he was young. Bron had done the carving, and his mother inlaid various stones. But within the frame was not a picture of anyone or anything. It was a piece of silky bark Sarala had beat and treated so it would last for years without chipping, breaking, or fading. Avid kept it blank for a long time, but in the last week he had written upon it:

I seek to love and serve the essence of life, the nectar of happiness, who is both within and without, near and far, self-illuminating and filled with love, the protector of animals and the giver of pleasure to all.

Under that, he had written his favorite instruction from his main teacher:

Love all beings and all things. Serve all and never exploit. Especially love the nectar seekers, whoever they may be and wherever they are. Love the sacred sounds and prayer. Love the teachers. Love sacred places. Love the path of love itself, which is surrender of all that is false and acceptance of devotion to all that is true. Have peace, forgiveness, and most of all, courage to conquer fear.

Avid wrapped the framed words in the lace and put it in a separate pocket in his pack. He then opened a drawer in which there was a carved box with a lock. Avid reached into a pocket in his pants for a key, and then unlocked the box and opened it. Inside there was a small bag of silk velvet, pulled tight with a string. Avid considered for a moment, opened the bag and removed what was inside. He took out a jewel which fit neatly into his hand and reflected every bit of light in the room. It was the color of dawn — a kind of orange-pink — which is the color of friendship with the Supreme Friend, herder of cows. It was a gift from his main teacher in Acumen. Or rather, his main teacher had taught Avid a way he could manifest the jewel from within his own heart. *I have my divine bee-like friend who is my guide, and I have the Supreme Friend, the Lord of All. And, my teachers in this world are my well-wishing friends. May I always serve all of them in gratitude!* Holding the jewel of spiritual service filled Avid's heart and whole being with a feeling of deep, intimate friendship with the cowherd. His desire to serve that Supreme Friend became so intense that Avid's body erupted in goosebumps, and tears streamed from his eyes. *I need to go.* He put the jewel in the bag and put the bag in a most secure inner pocket of his jacket.

He had maps and guidebooks handy in a pocket in his pack if he needed them. He had saved a fair bit of money, which went into its own smaller bag. Whatever he didn't pack was already given away, except for the empty carved box upon which he wrote the name of the landlord and "a gift for you." Otherwise the room was bare, but sparkling clean, when he handed the key to the landlord and started for home.

The day was beautiful, with just enough chill for the lightest of wools. Although he had completed his daily meditations and prayers, he still took out his beads and let his fingers roll each round piece of wood, smoothed and polished by many such rolling gestures. The chanted prayer repeated in his mind and slightly on his lips as he walked. In his walking meditation, he imagined an altar in his heart, where he invited the cow-herding, beautiful and all-attractive Lord of the Heart, the Soul of the Universe, The Supreme Friend, to sit on a diamond seat.

For lunch, he found a smooth rock under a tree to sit on, put away his meditation beads, and silently prayed another prayer of illumination and love. He brought out some of the food he had packed, plus fresh fruit he had picked from trees on the side of the road. As he ate, he sang, "I know that you will give protection to your treasured possessions, O Lord. I now understand the mentality of Your precious cows safely maintained by your side. You call your herds to pasture on the bank of the river by softly playing your flute. Fearless, and confident of your protection, I will drink that river water even when a poisonous snake has polluted it. Kindly protect me in the same way as you do your cows — with tender, loving care."

When he finished and washed his hands and mouth, he sang, "The Lord is my shepherd; I shall not want. He makes me to lie down in green pastures; He leads me beside the still waters. He restores my soul; He leads me in the paths of righteousness for His name's sake. Though I walk through the valley of the shadow of death, I will fear no evil; for you are with me; your rod and staff comfort me. You prepare a table before me in the presence of my enemies; my cup runs over. Surely goodness and mercy shall follow me all the days of my life; and I will dwell in your house forever."

As he walked, Avid again relished each word of both songs, feeling himself in a sort of walking, functional trance of loving contemplation, or samadhi. He was grateful for comfortable shoes. Yet when the brother of a friend he knew from Acumen offered a ride all the way to Dutiful, he accepted with equal gratitude. *I'm not sure whether I like it better to think of myself as the Lord's cow or the Lord's sheep.* He smiled at the humor of the thought, as he felt himself neither cow nor sheep. *He's my protector and maintainer, yes. Most of all, he's my friend — my dearest friend. I would love to play with him in divine pastures....* Avid fell asleep in the vehicle and woke in Dutiful. His driver offered to arrange a place for him to stay, and Avid agreed.

The problem with Dutiful, as Avid found in the morning, was not limited to the two witches that seemed to enchant most of the people there, but now only filled him with compassion when he saw them. Everyone was so... well, dutiful. Everyone felt it their duty to ask him his name, his father's name, his hometown, and his occupation. Most were scandalized that he was not married, and even more scandalized that he had studied in Acumen. "The place where lazy fools go to escape their duty," they called it. But they were pacified that he was traveling to attend his sister's wedding and please his father. "Father and mother are like God," they would say. "Family is like God." Avid found it hard to deeply meditate and pray there, even when he tried to do so in a few different buildings set aside for worship. *It is all so — what is that word my teacher used — fruitive. It's like a person who plants and cares for a tree only to get fruits. The only real purpose of their worship is getting from God a favorable result in this world for themselves or some sort of salvation. It's not really devotion. And their identity is entirely based in this world and worldly relationships.* He found people who sang the cowherd song, and others who sang the shepherd song, but somehow the way they sang it was odd. After a while he realized people sang those songs in order to protect their worldly possessions and social position or to assure their liberation. He was only too happy to leave Dutiful after two nights. The people he stayed with gave him a lot more traveling food, and in exchange he showed them how to create string and rope from twigs and leaves.

From Dutiful, the trip went quickly. He got several rides, the combination of which took him back to his parents' home. Duma welcomed him with tears mixed with laughter. "Finally! My son!" she said over and over. "Are you back to stay? There's a new family nearby with a lovely daughter just right for you, and you could work in Bron's store, now that you've got that journey out of your system."

Avid simply hugged her and wiped the tears from her face. "Momma, I'm here for Pena's wedding. Let me bathe and get something to eat." He then somehow extricated himself and went to his old room.

Even though he'd been gone only about a year, things seemed very different. Of course, Grandma was gone, and Mohah's child was walking around when they came to visit his parents' house — Avid was not welcome to visit Mohah, who acted like he was invisible. Sarala was expecting a baby. Pena was there with her fiancé, a decent and honest man, Avid decided after a week getting to know him. Tavis spent most of his free time in the forests and parks, and Duma's face looked like five years had passed since he saw her last. But it was not those changes that were the difference. It was him. Everyone, except Mohah, seemed really happy to see him. But Avid now had a daily routine of meditation, prayer, study, and worship. His family continued to follow the magic tradition which had brought them gold long ago, and they didn't understand his dedication or even his motives. Avid gradually did his Devotion Connection practices more and more privately, until everyone just thought he was waking up very late, rather than that he was involved in something strange early in the morning.

After a few days of unsuccessfully asking him to stay permanently, Duma begged Avid to stay for two months, although Pena's wedding was in only ten days, and he agreed. After the wedding, when Pena and her new husband said all the tearful good-byes and traveled to a distant village where they were going to live, Avid had some time to explore his home city without the pressures of school, job, or family responsibilities. Much to his surprise, he found small groups of people from the various schools in Acumen. *How strange that I had to go to Acumen in order to discover that such groups existed in my own home city! I guess we didn't know to look for them. We were so absorbed in our study in the library we thought we were the only ones in this city with such interests! Why should I be so surprised they are here? Acumen is mostly a city of schools, after all, and when people finish school, they often move on to live elsewhere.* Some of the groups were made of graduates from just one school within one discipline, and some were from mixed schools within a discipline. There were even two groups where the members were from various mixed disciplines. While Avid found those groups the most unusual and interesting, he joined a Devotion Connection group.

Avid started attending the meetings on Thursday nights, which promised talks of the spiritual world and the process of devotion. The gatherings would start with meditative group singing of prayers and mantras, and then a formal talk or discussion. Then, more singing, this time with dancing, and finally a meal. It was the meal that Avid soon found to be the problem, but not the meal itself as the food was amazing. The conversations at the meal were so different from the formal discussion before it, that it was as if he had gone to a different planet between those times. During the third meeting, Avid decided to speak to the couple who organized the meetings about the situation. "Thanks for having these gatherings," he started with.

"Oh yes, sure, Avid," the wife said, and both she and her husband stopped to give Avid their full attention.

"The singing, the formal talk, and the food are all—well, wow is the only word for it."

"You help contribute to the wow factor," the husband said as he mildly touched Avid on the shoulder.

"There's one thing that I'm wondering if we can do a little differently, though," Avid suggested. He saw the couple's smiles stop and noticed that the husband slightly raised his shoulders and stood a bit straighter. "Well see, you know it seems to happen every meal. In the formal talk we are speaking philosophy or about the Supreme Friend, the herder of cows."

"Yes, is that a problem?" asked the wife. She was looking around and was now giving Avid only part of her attention.

"No, no, not at all. The problem is, well, you see, when there is the meal, we relax. I know some groups eat in silence as a kind of discipline, and some only talk of high topics as we do in formal classes."

The husband replied, "You know, Avid, we have to take things slowly. Can't force or rush things. Everything in moderation. Loosen up and you'll do much better." His wife nodded at Avid and then walked away. He continued, "The stuff we talk about at the meal is just harmless socializing. Don't worry about it. See you next week," the husband said and followed his wife to the other side of the room to help with cleaning.

Avid tried for two more meetings. In the first of these, he got involved in the mealtime talk—talk of who got married, who got a job, and who died. They talked about the country's politics and the local and regional sporting events. To Avid it all felt empty and foolish, like hollow promises he had lost faith in long ago. Still, he had some trust in the couple who arranged the meetings, as they had been following a Devotion Connection path for much longer than he. So, he allowed his voice and his mind to flow along with the talk. Sometimes the talk would go into what various people in the city were doing wrong. Some of the "wrongs" were moral violations, and some were just the opinion of whoever was talking. Some of the people who were objects of criticism were in one of the connection schools — an essence seeker. When that happened, Avid would object. He had read and heard often enough that, except for emergencies, we should only correct others directly if they are under our care, or through proper channels if they are not, and always with respect. Especially, one should not look for faults with fellow essence seekers, no matter what school they were in or how advanced they were on the path. When he voiced an objection, others were dismissive of him much like the meeting organizer had been.

By the fifth meeting, Avid had accepted things and joined in all the mealtime conversations without objection. The next night he dreamed that he was walking down a street in the back areas of the city, after dark. In a doorway was a woman looking at him. As he looked back at her, he saw that her clothes were very tight and very short. She didn't dress or stand like the women he knew. In his dream, Avid felt his body respond to her as if she could pull him with animal-like attraction. He heard a voice in his mind — his divine bee-like friend — telling him to use his jewel. He felt for the jewel in his inner and outer pockets but it seemed to be gone. While he searched with more and more desperation, the woman called to him to come nearer. Then, suddenly in this dream, Avid was alone in his bed, all his possessions and money gone. He awoke from his dream in the middle of the night covered with sweat. Avid bathed and found his jewel of spiritual service in his jacket's inner pocket. He held it and felt the mood of sweet friendship fill him. As he put it away, he decided to spend extra time meditating that day. But, while he was meditating, he felt like he was in a vast desert. He had a vision of being hungry and thirsty, with no money and no friends. That day, he firmly resolved to find another group to meet with.

Ah, what a good decision it seemed at first! This other group was mostly from the Knowledge and Mastery Connection schools, with some people from the Action and Devotion schools. As a mixed group, they had meditations, philosophy, and discussions on practical application of work, in addition to prayerful song and dancing. Wonderful! Here the talk was never of worldly things. No one tolerated it at all. Their main focus was on gaining detachment and freedom. Avid felt renewed in spiritual strength.

One day, soon after Avid found the new group, he was sitting home with his mother. Duma started asking about his life, and brought up the same points she made before he went to Acumen. "Avid, what about a girl? You are making some money teaching forest craft, but you don't even have your own real place to live. What kind of future will you have?" she asked in question after question, not even pausing for Avid to answer.

"Mother—"

"You come and visit but you are in a worse situation than I imagined. You are spending most of your time away from your family, and not doing anything practical. How will you be a success?" *I'm losing my son. I've already lost him. I'm a failure as a mother. What is wrong with this boy?* "What can I do to get you to come back and have a real life?"

"Mother—mother! I'm a man now! Let me decide, please!" *Oh, the books warned of family attachment. She is so attached to me. Please, mother, stop asking useless questions, oh, stop.* "Mother!"

Duma started saying her rapid-fire questions louder and louder. Finally, Avid got loud with her, also, perhaps louder than he had ever spoken to her when he was growing up. Finally, Duma started crying and walked quickly out of the room.

Shaken, Avid went to an old favorite place in the adjacent forest. *I want to be free of family, of this world, and of all people! I want enlightenment and I want it now!* Avid threw some stones into the nearby stream and felt anger rise in his chest and stomach. *Why do I need to spend any time with family, anyway?* Soon, he heard the growl of a tiger. Looking carefully, he saw a tigress with cubs. She was fascinatingly beautiful.

When the stars threw down their spears
And water'd heaven with their tears:
Did he smile his work to see?
Did he who made the Lamb make thee?

Tiger, Tiger burning bright,
In the forests of the night:
What immortal hand or eye,
Dare frame thy fearful symmetry?

Avid became mesmerized and simply stared at the tigress. Ah, the hand of the Divine who made her and her cubs! What poetry in motion! What fierce elegance! Lost in thought and appreciation of her beauty, Avid—expert in forest craft that he was—forgot himself. But the tigress became aware of him. Generally, tigers do not attack humans, but the cubs were hungry. She watched and calculated the distance. Avid continued to watch her, almost spellbound and entranced. She crouched to strike, moving stealthily towards him. At that point, a second nature from all his years in the forest awoke. He realized that he was in imminent danger. Avid quickly stood up, put his hands high in the air and then wide, and took a deep breath. He made a lot of noise and moved his clothes to look very large. While doing that, he moved his feet quietly in a backwards walk. Still, the tigress was not deterred. *Ah, the jewel! I have a jewel!* Avid reached into his inside pocket and touched the jewel of his service to the Supreme Friend. Just touching it filled him with such feelings of friendship even in the moment of peril that he felt like his heart would burst with happiness. He pulled out the jewel and held it aloft where it caught the light of the setting sun and refracted it into the tigress' eyes. Simultaneously, a large rabbit crossed the path of the tigress. Distracted, she pounced on the rabbit and killed it. Avid ran fast for home while sometimes looking back, his life saved by his sacred jewel.

Calming down that evening, before the meeting, he read what he had written and framed. *Love, where is love? At these new meetings all they talk about is enlightenment, liberation, equilibrium, detachment, and freedom. That may seem better than the gossip in the other meetings. But, I am love and I want love. Love with the cowherd, my eternal protector. Oh, why did I not guard what I say and hear?* Avid skipped the meeting that night, packed early the next morning, wiped his mother's tears while hugging her, and walked to the main road.

That day, he got a message from Keen and Sage.

> Keen: Finding a connection between clay and spirit seems contradictory, but it's like the clay is my song and my speech to express my spirit."

> Sage: One night soon after you left, I was looking at my husband's sculptures — a lot like what you first saw so many years ago. I think something like what happened to you, happened to me. I started to remember, to feel, that I had been in each of those forms. They were memories, but not so much of what I did in those bodies, but more of what I felt. I could feel the longing for sunlight of the plants, the fear of the prey animal, and the bloodlust of the predator. Mostly, I felt varieties of hunger and fear.
>
> When the feelings subsided, my emotion turned to gratitude. So grateful to be human, to be able to think about higher topics, to have a clear sense of self, to know of death, and to know of the Divine.

Avid would have much to write to them of the next place he would travel through.

Love all beings and all things. Serve all and never exploit. Especially love the nectar seekers, whoever they may be and wherever they are. Love the sacred sounds and prayer. Love the teachers. Love sacred places. Love the path of love itself, which is surrender of all that is false and acceptance of devotion to all that is true. Have peace, forgiveness, and most of all courage to conquer fear.

Dissemble

While on the road, Avid sometimes walked alone, sometimes in a group, and sometimes he got a ride. He often took out his map to the Sacred Garden and rendezvous with the teacher. There seemed to be several routes to get there, and it wasn't obvious which one would be faster, or which would be a simpler journey. Avid decided to choose based on the rides offered to him, and places to stay along the way. Daily, he meditated on the mantra his main teacher had given him, and read about his beloved Lord, the sweet cowherd.

Other travelers said the easiest route to the Sacred Garden went through the town of Dissemble. He had been warned in Acumen to avoid the town, though he couldn't remember exactly why, and none of the other travelers seemed to have any idea. "Nice enough place," one gentleman said who had just come from there. "I can't imagine why anyone would tell you not to go there. Most of the folks there went to one of the schools in Acumen, they say. At least I can say that the people there seem serious about finding the essence of life."

After hearing such a description, Avid was more puzzled than before. *Why can't I remember what the problems are with that place?* However much he scanned his memory, he came up blank. *Well, whatever it is, it must not be too bad if I can't remember it.* He took a ride to Dissemble and resigned himself to whatever fate had in store for him.

Dissemble seemed like the most wonderful place! Sometimes it seemed to Avid as if the whole city were made of graduates from Acumen, and there were thousands of people who had taken some or all of the courses at Devotion Connection schools. Places of worship and devotional song were everywhere, and in the evening the streets filled with the most celestial and sublime singing and dancing. Avid found a place to stay near the edge of town, where he could walk to a particularly beautiful forest in only ten minutes. He decided that if he stayed a week, he could still easily catch up with his teacher and the group at the Sacred Garden.

The night he arrived, Avid was tired from his journey and went to bed very early. He had strange dreams of beasts whose masters pulled them with thick ropes as they carried heavy burdens. He woke a bit later than he usually did and saw that the sun was about to rise. Quickly, he washed, dressed, and did his sunrise meditation in his room. He read from the sheet he wrote in the frame, as well as from God's Song and other books, and then walked to the forest with his meditation beads and a small mat of woven reeds.

Fingering his beads and chanting softly as he walked, he felt the rays of the rising sun on his head. *The Soul of the World is the light of the sun, and the heat in fire. He is the purifying wind, and his artistic sense is evident in the beauty of the birds.* At this thought, pheasants ran across Avid's path, and he laughed quietly. Entering the woods, he found a smooth rock and put his mat upon it. Sitting straight, he breathed deeply using his diaphragm and got both relaxed and alert. *I am not Avid, not a human, not a man, not part of this world. I have no cares in this world. I let them go. I surrender myself to the one who is both within and without, near and far, self-illuminating and filled with love.* Avid closed his eyes and chanted on his beads, letting the sound of the holy name manifest the form of the Supreme Friend sitting on a diamond throne in his heart. Avid went so deep into meditation that he was there much longer than he had planned. The day turned to noon, and he had no awareness of the passing of time. Finally, after many hours, his focus broke and he opened his eyes. His inner peace remained, and he felt gently still. In front of him was his old and dear friend, his celestial bee-like guide. Around him, the forest and the whole world seemed frozen in movement and time.

"You have done well," the being said. "Beware this place. While truth is found in light, sometimes it is only in shadows that one finds what is hidden."

Avid communicated in thought — *I feel that I am finding the essence. May I call you friend, or should I call you teacher, or do you have a name? In Acumen I studied under a teacher who gave me a process, a prayer, and a jewel of service. But you are always my first teacher. And, this place seems wonderful, yet I will heed your warning.* Avid felt love for his guide swell in his heart. Although he didn't move, he felt as if he had risen from his seat and knelt at the feet of his guide, holding those feet to his forehead.

"Beware pride," the being said. "Pride breeds hypocrisy. When we find the essence and taste real sweetness in life, we will feel satisfied but never satiated. Love expands forever."

Avid still felt that he was lying prostrate on the ground, though he had not moved from his position even by a hair. Mentally he now got up and stood facing his friend. *Is it pride to say I am finding the essence? Yes? Well, then, the essence is finding me.* Avid felt that the being laughed gently without sound. *What should I call you? Friend?* A wave of peace washed Avid starting at the top of his head. *I guess that means yes, I can call you friend.* Another wave of peace mixed with joy filled Avid, this time starting in his heart and spreading outward. Then the being vanished, and Avid gradually stood up and looked around.

Back in the town of Dissemble, Avid got some lunch at a temple. The food was amazing in its variety, health, and taste. Then he went to a very large gathering for devotional singing, dancing, and a class. The class was wonderful! The speaker was full of enthusiasm, knowledge, and dedication. Avid spent time after the class talking with some of the other people, and he found none of the gossip and criticism he had encountered in the groups of his home city. There was not even talk of salvation separate from love. In other parts of the same building there were similar classes or singing going on, and Avid noticed that there was a lot of energy and enthusiasm in each group. He noted the faces of the leaders and how bright they were.

The program ended late, and Avid decided to walk around the town although it was dark. He still felt energized by his meeting with his bee friend in the forest and felt he could manage that night with less sleep than usual. As he meandered the streets, he noticed some strange and shocking sights. Well-dressed men and women with strangely twisted expressions and shining eyes were pulling people around with ropes around their necks. Those being pulled were protesting, and begging for release, but also looking adoringly towards their captors. The whole thing was so odd. Avid moved into the shadows to follow several such frightening processions. One of the odd-looking people, a leader perhaps, had ropes around the necks of several people at once. What was even more surprising, as he looked closely, was that some of the wonderful speakers he had heard that day had ropes around their necks.

One he followed entered a crowded restaurant and sat at a table that was already full of people. Along with his meal, he drank intoxicating beverages and started a loud argument. After watching for a while, Avid left. He then followed another man being pulled by a rope. That man entered a store, slipped some merchandise into his pocket, and quietly left without paying. For many hours Avid kept to the shadows—something he was good at from his forest craft training—and watched many people, men and women, get dragged into doing things which were the opposite of what those very people had been teaching earlier in the day. Finally, bewildered and exhausted, he went back to where he was staying and fell into a sleep troubled by dreams of twisted people yanking others around with intricate webs of ropes.

In the morning, Avid again got up later than usual. In his meditation on the Soul of the Universe, the Supreme Friend, the sweet cowherd—ah, such love—Avid felt he could forget everything in the world other than the Lord. He felt himself diving and surfacing in an expansive ocean of sweetness. As he focused on the mantra, thoughts of the form of the Lord and the activities of the Lord filled his heart, as if the highest heaven beyond the cosmos was within him. After breakfast, he pondered what he had seen the night before. It had been a very mysterious sight, indeed. Because a good number of the people he had seen bound at the neck were also speakers in the Devotion Connection meetings, he decided to find some of them and ask them what was going on.

Avid went to the building where he had attended the Devotion Connection meeting the night before. There was a reading room he hadn't noticed previously. It had God's Song and many other books, magazines, and pamphlets. Most of them he had read — some many times — and the majority of the rest were at least familiar. But his main purpose was to figure out how to contact those speakers. *Ah! Finally, here is a brochure with the names of speakers, with photos. This one! Yes, I saw him last night giving a class and later with a rope around his neck. Here's his name. No other contact information.* Avid took the brochure, got up, and went to see if anyone was in the building. From a woman organizing books, he got the address where the speaker worked during the day. *What, exactly, will I say to him? That I saw an odd-looking man pull him by a rope into a shop where he stole something? How will I start such a conversation?*

On the way to the address, Avid walked down a street he had traveled on his first day in Dissemble. He noticed how artistic and elegant the buildings looked. They appeared to be very old and created by master artisans. On a whim, he entered one building whose exterior was particularly striking. Inside, however, it appeared to be both recently built and of shoddy materials. The floors were imitation wood, and the walls were unpainted plaster. The furniture looked like a young child had made it, and stains were here and there on the upholstery. Bewildered, Avid quickly left. Back on the street he noticed several of the trees, tall and wide, shading the walkway. He walked over to one of them. His Devotion Connection practices had honed his awareness of how to sense the life, the being in the body of a tree, with a dim recollection that he had himself been in such a body long out of any conscious memory. As he came near, he felt a wave of pain as if the tree was cramping. Shocked, he touched the tree and stroked its bark. Some large pieces of bark came off in his hand, and he could tell that the heart of the tree was rotting from some sort of disease. As he empathically connected to the tree, he could sense the web of communication the trees shared underground through their roots and through fungi, and he suddenly sensed that most of the trees were similarly rotting in their heartwood.

The experience with the trees filled him with a tired sadness. *I need to find a place to sit. Perhaps in that building.* There was another building, again with a stunning exterior. But, again, when he went through the door, it was clear that the building was recently built and of the cheapest materials with barely skilled labor. *The outside is just a façade, and probably not real stone.* He tapped on the outside and heard a hollow sound. *A resin mixture to imitate stone.*

The nature of Dissemble was becoming apparent, and Avid felt less need to speak to the man he was seeking. But, having started on the mission, he decided that there was no harm in completing it. After an hour of walking through similar streets, he finally reached the address. It was now time for lunch, and Avid hoped the place had some meals available.

Avid found Lajja — for that was the man's name — in a huge office with hand-carved furniture made of rare woods. At least it appeared so, for Avid was now skeptical of anything in this town. Nothing was what it appeared. Intricate paintings of spiritual subjects graced every wall, and a secretary asked Avid to wait for a short time until Lajja finished some other work. Thankfully, he brought Avid a light meal to eat during the wait.

Lajja graciously offered Avid a seat on a plush, comfortable chair. He himself moved from behind his desk to sit on a similar chair facing Avid. *He does not want to appear as some big authority, but more like a friend. There is good in him.*

"So, how may I render some service to you, young man?" Lajja offered.

"I attended your lecture last night," Avid started, trying to smile.

"Ah, and did you like it?"

"Yes, very much. Very much indeed. I felt energized." Avid looked at his hands and at the desk. "But, well, I wasn't very tired afterward." *Why am I even talking to him at all? This is crazy.* "You see, well, I took a walk around town until pretty late."

"That's not a very good idea. We are advised to sleep early and wake early for spiritual life."

"Yes, well, yes, that is true. But you see, I saw something very odd and I'm wondering if you could help me to make sense of it."

"Yes?" Lajja turned to look at Avid fully and intently. "I don't have much time, young man, but I can try to help."

"I... I saw you stealing, sir, and, and, well, you had a rope around your neck. Someone very strange-looking was dragging you." Avid felt his face turn several shades of red and the clothing under his arms get wet. "I don't take anything that clouds the consciousness, sir, as I'm a student of the Devotion Connection and under firm vows. I swear that I saw this and I would like to understand it."

Lajja continued looking intensely at Avid for a while, and then leaned back in his chair. "You must have mistaken me for someone else, young man—what is your name?"

"Avid, sir."

"Yes, Avid. I go to sleep early. So, it must have been someone else. But, I have heard such stories before. Yes, indeed I have. There are enemies in this town, nasty enemies. And they ensnare and pull people around to get them to do things they should not do."

"Who are these enemies?"

"I'm not sure, but I heard—perhaps you have read?"

Lajja spoke long but without substance. Avid felt his mind wandering from what Lajja was saying. Lajja stopped looking directly at Avid, and Avid took the opportunity to look around the room while Lajja was speaking. He noticed various pictures around the room. Many seemed to be of Lajja's family, and his Devotion Connection teachers. But there was another picture on a bookcase, high on a shelf, but in a gorgeous frame. It was a small picture, but even from where he was sitting, Avid could clearly see that the person in the picture was the man with the distorted face Avid had seen dragging Lajja around. *Ah, it's our own lust, our own greed, our own anger...we cannot identify those who drag us with ropes because they are dear to us!* Lajja continued to talk about being careful on the devotional path. Finally, he paused to take a breath.

"Yes, thank you, sir. Thank you, Lajja. I think I understand now. We keep dear to us the very things which damage us."

"Yes, that is correct. Good, good, though I don't think I got to that point yet. You already understand. Yes, such is a problem among many in our community. Stay away from such people."

"Indeed, I will, Lajja sir. Thank you for your time." Avid quickly got up and left.

Just to check that he had not been imagining anything, Avid rested during the day and again walked around Dissemble at night. This time he realized that there were only about ten of the strange twisted people who carried ropes yet they seemed to be able to pull hundreds of people in hundreds of directions at a time. In one sense, each person had their own individual variation of the ten twisted people. Often, the twisted people were pulling those who spoke wonderfully about connection and inspired others. Those being pulled with a rope acted against the very principles they taught.

Finally, most the people of Dissemble went to their homes to bed, and the ten or so twisted people came together for a very late night—really very early morning—drink and meeting. Avid was able to sit in a dark corner of the place to watch and listen.

"Heh, it was so easy to get that one! You said it would be hard, Envy, but it was easy!"

"I never said it would be hard for you, Fear. Anyway, as long as one of us gets 'em, doesn't matter much who it is!"

"I saw Anger very active tonight," Fear responded, looking at another twisted person.

"You accusing me of something?"

"No, just enjoyed the big fight," Fear answered.

"I had fun in the entertainment palace," another answered.

"Humph," responded Envy. "Hey, Lust, I saw three people—three!—escape you tonight, and I'll place my bets that it was for good. I saw the sign."

"Look, none of us can do much when they call for help properly to the right people, Envy. Not even you. Losing some is just part of the game."

"Yeah, Envy!" Anger answered. "I saw five people—not three—get free of your ropes tonight."

"Ah, true, true," Envy said. "I will not deny it. But only two of them humbly called for help from the guides. The others will be back in a few days or weeks. You can be sure of that."

"Let's drink to that!" they all said in unison and clanged their glasses together.

Avid felt fear and anger well inside his own body. Anger that these twisted people would capture so many good souls, and fear that it might happen to him. *I've a right to feel these things. These people are horrible. I've a right. If I don't feel this way, then it means that I'm wrong.* Pride then rose within him. He could feel fear, anger, and pride grow within his heart area and move throughout his body. *I've a right! These people are horrible. I must stop them!* Avid stood up and started to move towards them, intending to fight with them, yell at them, and maybe hit them. As he did so, he became aware that he was not moving under his own power, as if something was pulling him against his will from around his neck. He stopped for a tiny fraction of a second and felt around his neck. "Be gone, thieves!" he whispered but to no avail. He grabbed for the jewel of service. It sparkled and seemed to softly sing that he needed more. *The guides—who are the guides they spoke of?* "My teacher who gave me the jewel of service and my mantras! And, also, my friend! My bee-like, nectar-drinking friend! Save me!"

Slowly, although he was not in any forest, he could feel the presence of his divine bee-like friend, the nectar seeker. He could hear the voice of his friend in his mind. "Avid, watch the anger, fear, and pride come and go. Do not give them a safe harbor. Just watch. Watch the feelings and laugh at them. Do not hold them, and do not hate them. You are not them. Who should be in your heart? Put him there."

Suddenly, Avid could feel how he was the observer, the spirit, and not the mind or body. He watched the feelings and thoughts with curiosity and amusement but focused his thoughts on the beautiful cowherd in his heart. "The Lord is my shepherd. I shall not want." And the ropes were gone, the feelings retreated. Avid quickly left the place and returned to his room to sleep a bit until the dawn.

As he got into the bed, he noticed a message from Keen and Sage:

Keen: We are getting anxious for the baby to be born. I have been thinking a lot about how much of a debt of gratitude we owe our teachers on this path. I follow on a map where you are and join you in spirit.

Sage: The sense of gratitude after my experience with my husband's clay figures has stayed with me, though it's not as powerful now. I tried to explain everything to Keen. It's funny that he makes those clay creatures, but he never traveled into them as you and I have. How odd that often what we are closest to we perceive differently than those who have a little distance. Every day my thoughts fill more and more with the baby inside me, and I hope he or she will also feel the gratitude that seems to swell and flow within me.

Avid thought about his friends and their life in Acumen as he fell asleep, but a strange dream of donkeys woke him unusually early.

Donkeys by the Sea

The next day Avid found a group of people going to the Sacred Garden and decided to travel with them. They all left soon after breakfast. The group consisted of about ten people, mostly married couples, some with children. Two of the single people had grown up in Dissemble and were leaving permanently, whereas the rest had passed through like Avid. All but one person had studied in Acumen. They were traveling on foot with a few wheeled carts to carry heavy things, as they felt foot travel was more appropriate for a pilgrim's journey than vehicles. Avid wasn't sure he agreed, but they were excellent company and he didn't mind walking. He felt certain he would meet up with the Acumen teacher and group without trouble.

By the end of the day, the group had shared their own experiences of the twisted people with ropes in Dissemble. Everyone in the group — except the very young children — had seen the twisted people at least once, and everyone had felt a rope around his or her own neck. When Avid mentioned that he got free by calling for help from his friend and guide, the others were interested and related similar stories.

"I remembered my main teacher in Acumen — the one who gave me my prayers and mantras," said Avid, "and I also called for a special friend and guide who has been with me for many years. I had to admit that I needed help. And I got it."

"I think that the main thing is admitting the need for help from a qualified guide," one woman suggested as she adjusted the baby she carried on her back. Everyone nodded.

Avid was impressed that the group had provisions for camping as they traveled. He had brought only minimum gear, but with his advanced forest craft he was able to be of so much use to everyone that one unmarried man about his age happily shared his tent and supplies with Avid. Unlike Avid, he hoped to marry, but he wanted to spend time in the Sacred Garden first.

After a few days of traveling with no villages in sight, they came to the town of Jennyville. Here, they were just a two-week journey away from the Sacred Garden. At least there were signs to that effect by all the main entrance points. Avid wasn't sure if the signs meant two weeks' journey by foot, or riding a horse, or going in a vehicle!

At first sight, Avid liked Jennyville better than any place he had visited, perhaps even Acumen. It was next to a freshwater sea, with many rivers and waterfalls coming down from nearby mountains. A light rain was falling when they arrived, which combined with sunshine to produce double rainbows in various directions. The leaders of the group had pre-arranged a sanctuary where the whole group would stay. Avid found a spot for his pack, bathed, and walked to where he could gather food from the lush forest with a view of the sea. *No need to cook in this city. I can offer my food to my dearest Lord and eat it raw.* Avid ate alone, and then, as he did daily, meditated on the holy name for several hours, his consciousness absorbed in the transcendent realm.

Avid sent messages to each of his family members—even Mohah—and answered new messages from Keen and Sage. Their art business was doing well, and Keen was training to be an assistant teacher in the Devotion Connection school. Sage was in good health and happy to welcome their newborn son. They each wrote that they traveled with Avid in spirit.

The group Avid had come with was staying a few days and Avid decided to attend some programs of singing and classes by Devotion Connection leaders. What a joy the meeting was! The speaker, who reminded him strongly of his grandma though she was considerably younger, spoke about loving service, but also about the twisted people who drag us around with ropes on our necks! Avid was thrilled to find someone talking openly about this, and he listened carefully.

After the talk, more singing, and a light meal, Avid sat for a while with the speaker. They spoke of the ropes pulling otherwise sincere people to foolish action. "Hypocrites," Avid said. "But you had a rope around your neck, too, didn't you?" the teacher softly said, while her eyes smiled. "Are you, or were you, a hypocrite?"

Avid looked her straight in the eyes and smiled gently. "Well, I guess so, yes?"

They both laughed and spoke about the stories of the cowherd. "Are you going to the Sacred Garden?" the woman asked.

"Yes, and I'm excited and not sure what to expect."

"Expect to find the essence of life, the real nectar. Of course, the Sacred Garden is with us all the time, if we open ourselves to it." She paused and looked at the various people talking and going home. "Yet, it helps to go there also. I have been many times. Your name is —?"

"Avid."

"Ah, Avid, watch where you bathe in Jennyville. Always be aware of how you feel. Those who bathe in the ocean of love always feel joyful and peaceful. Be aware. There is a type of hypocrite who fools himself."

"Thank you. I will." Avid got up, bowed slightly before he realized he was bowing, and left for the sanctuary to rest for the night. Although it was late and dark, no matter where he wandered, he saw no twisted people with their ropes.

In the morning, Avid woke earlier than usual and decided to take his morning bath in the freshwater sea, which residents called the ocean of love. The sun had not yet risen but silhouettes in the pre-dawn light allowed Avid to travel easily. While he had been close to the sea already, he had not gone to a place where one could swim, and found that the path to the swimming area was very different than the way he had taken when he had gathered fruits and meditated. Evidently it was not as easy to bathe in the ocean of love as to admire it.

Avid came to a fork in the path. A large, ferocious beast sat as if guarding one of the paths. Avid took the other, unguarded path. Quickly, that path became dusty, with flowering invasive plants growing along the sides of the road. *These plants require no care but they take over everything. Although they do produce flowers, the flowers smell like rotten cabbage and the leaves give you a rash.* There were groups of people singing on benches or mats in shady areas. Their songs were of devotion, but their voices were harsh and grating. A little further ahead a group of people was having a heated argument over some philosophical point, and one man looked like he was about to cry, whereas another stood over him with crossed arms and chin high, looking smug. A strange smell was getting ever stronger.

There was a sign, "Bathing Area Ahead," which was a relief as Avid was starting to feel very sweaty and wanted to get away from the smell. As he approached the bathing area, however, the smell only got stronger. There were also patches of what looked like burnt vegetation. Another sign, "Bathing Area," was just up ahead. By this time the smell was almost unbearable, and Avid covered his nose and mouth with a cloth.

Huge donkeys were standing near the edge of a rock ledge, urinating. The urine poured over bathers who were singing, "Ah, we are cleaning our minds!" The urine was so acidic that it had burned places in the rock, and the skin of some of the bathers was covered in rashes. Some of the people he had seen at the talk, and even one from his traveling group were there.

Avid couldn't contain himself. "That's donkey urine!" he almost shouted, running over to one of the bathers and pushing him out of the way. "You are burning. And stinking. What are you doing?"

The bather got very annoyed. "These, dear visitor, are streams from the ocean of love. Our minds are purified by these charming waters. Don't push me, and get out of my way!"

Avid quickly moved away and started running down the path back to the fork. On the way, there were several groups of people. Many were clearly angry at each other, and there were shouting matches. Avid could clearly hear one woman yelling, "I'm doing this for love! It's spiritual! What's the matter with you? I am pure and clean! Why do you question my motives? You are full of envy!" He ran even faster and returned to the fork in the path and the beast, who was resting in the light of the rising sun.

At this point, Avid was sweaty and dusty. *Maybe I should just bathe in the bathing room where I am staying? But that woman told me to bathe in the ocean of love. Maybe I can sneak past the beast.* Avid used all his forest skills, and started to walk on the narrow area between the impenetrable hedges on either side and the sleeping huge beast.

The beast's roar startled Avid. He felt two things at once: great fear and the presence of his celestial bee friend, along with the usual stillness. His friend's voice echoed in his mind, though Avid could not see him. "Courage, Avid! The Beast of Fear wants you to look at your mind. Why do you want to travel to the Sacred Garden?"

Avid spoke both to his bee-like friend and to the beast in thought, avoiding the beast's stare. *I... I seek truth. I seek the essence. In the Sacred Garden that essence is available in abundance even on the surface.*

"Look in your mind, Avid," said his nectar-seeking friend. "Ask the cowherd, supreme ruler and friend of all, my dear one and master. Ask him! Ask him to show you what is really in your mind!"

I am afraid.

"Ask for courage, then!"

"Dear Supreme Friend, dear cowherd, dear Soul of the Universe, who is near and far, within and without, please show me the real state of my mind, and give me courage to see it and make the right choices."

The beast moved aside and lay down again. Avid thought he sensed the beast's satisfaction, but he couldn't be sure. *Ah, now that the beast has moved a bit, I can see that there is the ocean of love at the end of this path!* Avid ran to it, took some of its water in his palms and splashed it on his face. A very quiet voice, full of love yet serious, spoke distinctly but not audibly in the physical sense. "Avid, this is the ocean of our love. Are you ready to know the real motives in your mind?"

Avid had a surety that this voice was that of the cowherd, Soul of the World, Supreme Friend. He answered in thought, as he did with his divine bee guide. *Yes.* He stood up at the shore and closed his eyes. He entered a state of relaxed alertness. He soon felt that he was in the audience of some sort of performance. But on the stage were bits of his own life. He saw himself seeming to act righteously and caringly, but motivated by pride or greed. He could feel the pain, humiliation, and hurt others felt from his own actions — actions he told himself at the time were coming from his adherence to duty or protection or some worthy intention. *Ah, now I understand the donkey urine bath! I thought I was cleaning my mind in all those actions but I was only externally doing the right thing. Sometimes even externally I wasn't really doing the right thing at all. Excuses, rationalizations. Oh, how foolish!*

"Are you ready to let go?" the clear yet inaudible voice asked.

Avid felt deep shame and grief. *Yes, yes. I am ready.*

Then warnings from voices very different from that of the cowherd, but also inaudible but clear, rushed in from all directions as if they were a gang trying to rob him. These voices were not loving and serious, but felt very urgent, like strangers advising caution. Maybe they were his own thoughts, and maybe they were distinct entities, like some sort of monsters. He heard: "If you let go of those motives, you will become irresponsible. You'll lose your incentives for action. You'll be useless. Anyway, it's too hard. You've seen so many fail. How do you imagine you can let go?"

Avid felt fear and hopelessness. Then, again, he witnessed the pain he was causing to himself and others from deceptive motives. He listened for the voice of serious love, who he felt sure was the cowherd himself, but there was silence. This was a choice he had to make himself. *Yes, yes. No matter what the price. Let any terrible things happen, but let my mind be clean. I trust you, cowherd. Oh, fearful thoughts or monsters or whatever you are — be gone!*

Suddenly, a great wave came from the ocean of love and gently knocked Avid down. It covered him and swirled around him. Not only were the fearful thoughts gone, but also gone were the selfish and evil motives in his mind. He knew with absolute certainty that he was free from those motives forever. While even his clothes had gotten wet, Avid felt refreshed and as if he was a new person. His mind filled with peace and joy beyond understanding or description. *I am free. I am free. Surely I have found the essence and there is nothing better than this!* Avid swam in the sea for what seemed like hours and then returned to his room.

A Dead Dog

The group soon journeyed onwards to the Sacred Garden, and
Avid now felt his mind often filling spontaneously with the stories and moods he had studied and read about, whereas previously he made deliberate efforts to remember them. It was as if
the Sacred Garden and the ultimate world were starting to grow
within him. When he meditated on his mantra, he started to see
not only the beautiful cowherd, but also himself. He could tell
that his original nature, fully spiritual, had a form. That form
was not of flesh and blood, nor did it have the limitations of mundane forms. It seemed to him that forms of this world were some
sort of imitation. He could feel a budding of emotions of friendship with the Supreme Soul, and he spent as much time as possible reading the books that would help with his own mood.

It was a wonderful group to travel with, but Avid noticed that
the person he'd seen bathing in donkey urine had not come with
them. Since he had left the ocean of love, he had been confronted
again by the image and feeling of the beast and the clear instruction to open his mind with courage. He was learning how to sub-
mit his mind like an open book to the Soul of the Universe, who
showed him a fault masquerading as a virtue. Then his mind (or
the monster voices?) would present fears, and Avid would feel
himself swimming in the ocean of love and having the fault removed. This process happened many times, while he was walking or eating or meditating. It could come at any time. It was
quite wonderful.

In fact, it was so wonderful that Avid came to feel as if a

waterfall of the ocean of love was constantly cascading from the heavens, surrounding him with a golden light. Little by little, he felt as if his mind was always swimming in the ocean of love. The world around him appeared to be merely shadows, a wonderful energy of illusion which he appreciated more and more but with less and less desire to try to exploit or enjoy. Hardly anything in the world attracted or disturbed him, and he felt like he floated effortlessly instead of walking or riding.

Others in the group noticed the change in Avid, and quite a few people quietly asked him if he had bathed in the ocean of love. "Yes," he would always answer truthfully. Sometimes he would add, "I'm bathing all the time." He felt his heart swell, knowing he was achieving all he sought when he had first left home with Keen and Sage. In fact, he sent them a message gushing about what he was experiencing, and how it was changing his life. Keen wrote back briefly saying how happy he was for Avid, and Sage wrote that she was experiencing something similar which she would explain later. Avid really felt that he was on the right track, and was filled with a peace and happiness he had only dreamed of before. Avid noticed that his fellow travelers started to treat him with increasing respect. At every small town where they stopped, people often gave him special food and fancy places to stay. He could hear them whispering that he was a saint. In one town, people washed his feet and drank that water, hoping for a blessing. *This is embarrassing, but after all my searching and study and daily practice of meditation, why shouldn't people respond to my dedication to the path?*

Avid sat outside in one of these towns in the evening, absorbed in his meditation and almost unaware of the world around him. He felt no cares, no worries, no anxieties about anything. He barely felt that he had a human body. As he finished his meditation and opened his eyes, he saw many of the creatures of the park and nearby forest gathered around him. *They can tell who swims in the ocean of love. I have achieved all I desire, and naturally others notice. It's not pride; what can be done?* Avid stroked the creatures, internally singing his favorite song. Whenever he sang that song, he felt as if he were running in the fields of the spiritual world with the Soul of All, the cowherd.

Avid decided to wander around the town a bit before returning to where he was staying. Because this town was very near to the Sacred Garden, most people there were from one of the Devotion Connection schools. Many of them also had minds swimming in the ocean of love—it was easy for Avid to recognize someone like that—and, in general, most people there seemed fairly advanced in the process over all. He felt as if he was with extraordinarily kindred souls with whom he could discuss the most inner longings of his heart. They spoke of their realized relationships with the cowherd, Supreme Friend and Soul of the World.

As he walked in the warm night, many open doors brought the sweetest sounds of devotional singing into the street. There were also dancing groups going through the street, singing to the one beloved of all as they moved in unison. He joined some of the groups for a while as he went to his destination. He felt as if his feet didn't even touch the ground.

The next day at lunch he sat with some people from his group, along with some from the town. The meal was simple—bean soup, salad, and bread. During the meal, someone from his group told those from the town, "And Avid here—he joined us a while ago—always has his mind swimming in the ocean of love. His purity and devotion are unmatched."

"Ah, very wonderful!" said a young boy of perhaps twelve years.

The boy's father smiled at his son. "It's important to be able to recognize saintly persons. Saintly persons open for us the door to perfection."

"I'm trying to follow my teachers," Avid replied as he had been taught, as if by rote, and he looked around. *Yes, they are right. I am, indeed, always swimming in the ocean of love in my mind. I am free from the ropes of lust and anger. My speech is pure, free of the harlot of gossip and the tiger of desire for loveless salvation. Why shouldn't they recognize me? It's not pride to be happy that they are speaking truth.* As he looked around, everyone was smiling and nodding. Then he looked down at his plate.

Instead of salad and bread, he saw a rotting carcass of a dog! Avid nearly jumped out of his seat. *What is this? How did my food turn to this? Why doesn't anyone else notice? Oh, my bee-like friend, show me the truth, explain this meal, and give me courage!* Stunned by the spectacle, Avid stopped eating and willed his face and hands to remain relaxed so no one else would sense anything strange. Others started talking about the upcoming journey and he was able to listen silently, hoping no one noticed he was not eating.

Avid heard his divine friend and sensed the presence but saw no one. "Avid, this problem cannot be solved in the same way as we did with the mind, which was full of selfish motives for good actions. I will show you your heart, wherein is the root of ego and pride."

While Avid sat at the table, seeming to listen to the conversation, his awareness traveled far away. He was in a dark place lit with red-colored lights. "You are in the heart," his friend's voice reverberated in his consciousness. "Watch and feel." Avid saw, again, the dead dog on a plate before him, and also saw that there was a man and woman in the room. They were dancing together in a strange and sensual way, trying to draw everyone's eyes to them. The man was wearing a mask, which at various points in the dance he changed for yet another and another. The woman would stop dancing for a moment to take a bite of the dog carcass, or to grab the hands of various men in the room and pull them onto the dance floor with her. Then she would return to her original partner. After some time, she took Avid's hands and brought him to the floor. Without words, she clearly asked him to dance and to taste the dead dog with her. Avid seemed to dance with her effortlessly, though some part of him wondered why. As he touched her hand, he could feel the energy she experienced by all eyes riveted on her, appreciating her expert dancing. And, then he understood who she was and what the dead dog was.

Avid was suddenly back in the room with his fellow travelers and newly met townsfolk. Remorse, shame, and humility flooded his heart, but combined with a sweetness beyond what he had experienced previously. He stood and left the table, getting some pamphlets from his bag in the other room. He returned and gave one to each of the other people there. "Here is a small pamphlet that my main teacher in Acumen wrote," he told them. "Whatever you may find of value in me is because my teacher is kind to me. I'm going to the Sacred Garden because one of my other teachers in Acumen invited me, and my main teacher agreed. I'm hoping I can serve my teachers by going there."

Avid sat back down and looked at his plate. The contents had returned to salad, bread, and soup. He sighed and finished the meal. He quickly excused himself and went to his room. The next day they would travel the last leg to the Sacred Garden.

In his room, he opened his teacher's pamphlet and started to read, "A loyal and humble student…" The words blazed as if imbued with light and power beyond anything Avid could have imagined. Each word was full of power and freedom. He felt himself lifted beyond a veil of illusion, beyond anything he could understand. Love flooded his every particle of existence. He felt like he could taste humility, and that humility was like a spice added to the ocean of love which imparted a further indescribable taste, as if made up of a combination of every wonderful flavor. Aliveness pulsated around him, and he felt fully himself in his eternal spiritual identity. In that state, song and prayer flowed from him effortlessly, and it was deep into the night before he slept.

The next day, he got a message from Sage that moved him to tears:

> After I shared this with Keen, he urged me to tell you also. So, I'm going to try my best…You'll think it's really strange how it… I don't know what to call it… happened to me. Each school has a name for it, and the names are useful but they

don't really describe — can't describe — what it is. Before the baby was born, when I had sold a lot of my textile art, and a few pieces of my husband's work, a very old woman entered the studio. She looked so old that for a moment I had a thought that it's a cruelty that she was still living in such a broken-down body, and then felt immediately guilty that such had crossed my mind.

The woman went directly to some of Keen's sculptures about our ultimate friend, the cowherd. Usually we don't allow anyone to touch the art, but somehow when she stroked the clay, I remained respectful. Suddenly, Avid, and maybe you won't believe this but it's true, I could feel the divine presence of the cowherd in the studio. Oh, Avid, he is so beautiful! I felt as if all my senses were eyes to see his beauty, and then I started to feel faint due to the intensity. Then, I smelled something beyond roses, or jasmine, or ylang-ylang, or gardenia, or anything I have ever smelled. My heart almost broke from the joy of that smell, and all my senses felt they could smell the scent. Again, I was overwhelmed, and then I felt his touch. Yes, Avid, his touch! Softer than butter, smoother than velvet, more delicate than silk, more comforting than the embrace of who we love the most (sorry, dear Keen). All my senses became touch receptors and I forgot where I was and my name. Then, the sound! Oh, Avid, the sound of his voice is like thundering clouds yet gentle like a father holding a two-year-old on his lap. "Do not fear," he said, and such a peace was in me.

I don't know how it happened, dear Avid, but I let go. I let go of trying to control anything, or even to be anything. I let go of what anyone might think or say. I trusted. It's a gift, Avid. All our spiritual practices are only helping us to be receptive to acceptance of ourselves, but we earn nothing. It is the gift of the one who is near and far, who is within us and besides us, and the gift of the teachers he sends us. He is love!

Garden of Sacred Fragrance

As they came to the gates of the Sacred Garden, Avid felt some disappointment. The town seemed very old and in poor repair. He entered with the group he had been traveling with, and then left them once he was inside the gates — with many thanks and some tears — to find Ucitel, the teacher from Acumen, and his group. Although Ucitel's group was small, he himself was well-known, and Avid found them in less than an hour.

"Avid! Avid! I have so often thought of you but I never got a way to message you before you left Acumen. I wondered if you would actually come!" Ucitel smiled broadly. Avid offered his respects and sat on a mat on the floor along with the others. "I know I'm not your main teacher. The teacher who taught you your prayers and meditations is doing well. I hope I can serve you here."

"How long have you been here, and how much longer are you staying, Sir?" Avid asked, so happy and relieved to have arrived.

"Our classes in Acumen start in two months, so we will stay six weeks more. We have been here three weeks already. Go with one of the others around the town. Remember that this is a dhahm, higher than a portal. But you need the password to see it and feel it."

"The password?" Avid asked, puzzled, but Ucitel was already talking to his other students. Avid shrugged and decided to find some others with whom he could explore. He quickly found three people he knew well from Acumen who agreed to take him in the afternoon. In the meantime, he went to a quiet spot outside with a pleasant breeze and studied.

In the afternoon, as Avid walked through the Sacred Garden with the others, his initial impression kept being confirmed. Every building was old, with plaster missing in places, rotted wood, and well-worn stone steps. He did not see any glorious opulence as he had hoped and expected. As he gradually drew his attention away from the buildings, he noticed that the residents of the town had obviously all studied in Acumen, and they sang as they walked, although their walking seemed almost like dancing. Parrots of many colors flew in pairs from tree to tree, and peacocks danced for peahens. Much of the place was agricultural fields. Domestic animals of all types — dogs, cats, goats, sheep, buffalo, and cows — wandered in those fields, healthy and well-fed. His group took him through those fields to forests. "You need the password to enter," the leader of his group told him in an offhand way while checking something in his bag.

"Why can't we just enter?" Avid asked, confused.

"Ok, we can take you into the forest, but I doubt we will actually enter in the real sense," the leader replied while checking the time and getting the group together.

"As you like," Avid replied and followed, even more confused. *I wonder if he knows anything about passwords and forests. He seems to be telling me something memorized that he doesn't believe.*

What the guide called a "forest" was not much of a forest by Avid's definition. There were small, twisted trees covered with thorns. The trees were so short that they provided no shade and the sun felt hot. Forest litter — dried leaves, dead insect bodies, pieces of wood, and so forth — covered the rocky and sandy ground under the trees. Small creatures such as squirrels and rabbits scuttled out of the way. At one point they came to a clearing of sorts, where there was mostly sand dotted with thorns and rocks. The group stopped to rest and eat some crackers and fruit. Avid wasn't hungry, and wandered a little distance away. He saw some flowers — the first he had seen that day — and among them many bees. Avid squatted down to observe the bees closely. As had happened so many times before, everything became silent and still. Time seemed to stop. He lost the desire to move even slightly. Soon, his divine friend became somewhat visible, although Avid could never really make out his friend's form.

"Avid, Avid, why aren't you asking for the password?"

Avid remembered what both the teacher and group leader had said. At the time, their talk of a password just seemed odd and he had not let the thought sit in his mind. *Yes, I want the password. Is it only a word? What does it do? I don't understand.* Avid could feel the peace of the stillness and silence as if it was a soft, thick, and comforting blanket. He waited, open and willing.

"It is not only a word in the ordinary sense, Avid. It is the name of the Supreme Friend, your friend! The cowherd! And, yet, not a name. A name in this world is a provisional sound attached to a person or object, but without any real relation to what or who it names. One could call the same object or being any number of things and there would be no real change. The password is not a name of this world. It is a holy name you have said so many times, thousands or millions, Avid. You have meditated on the holy name and tried with effort to realize the name's glories. The password means to fill your heart with that name, as if you had an internal throne of friendly affection for the name to sit on and reveal himself to you. The name should go in your ears, sit in your heart, and then move to your tongue. Then, you will feel the name dancing on your tongue. That dancing will fully reveal your own nature and destroy all illusion. The forest will then reveal itself to you."

Avid listened carefully. *I have tried, dear friend and teacher, numerous times to do exactly what you are describing.* He sighed without moving his chest or shoulders.

"Yes, I know. But you have already let go of so much, Avid, so you have the wisdom and courage to let go of the rest. Furthermore, you are in the Sacred Garden. All effort has a thousand times the strength here."

Avid smiled without facial movement. *All right, I will make my best attempt.* Avid again sighed although his chest and shoulders remained still.

Avid mentally said the holy name, the name of his ultimate friend, the Soul of the World, the cowherd, who is the essence of life, the nectar of happiness, what is both within and without, near and far, what is self-illuminating and filled with love. He said the name with all the friendship he could allow to flow from his heart, but without any expectation, just giving and surrender.

Avid then felt the source of his reluctance to fully love and surrender. His mind was filled with fear of loss. *We are more afraid of losing something we have, than of not gaining something we want or need.* He could feel and almost see the fear of loss of self-centeredness, of autonomy. There was a fear of scarcity and privation, a fear of loneliness. Fear of pain and disability hovered around him. He could feel the fears as if they were a crowd of people, each with a different weapon and threat, gradually closing in upon him in a circle.

"You have the jewel of spiritual service. You have the protection of the great teachers. You can swim in the ocean of love. You found humility in your loyalty to your teachers. Use what you have!" the nectar-seeking divine bee said, audible only to Avid.

In his mind, Avid felt for the jewel of service he kept in his pocket. He felt himself taking it out of the pocket and bag, though his physical hand did not move. The jewel shone with a dazzling light, illuminating the circle of fear around him. In the full light, he could immediately understand that all the fears were superficial, only façades, without substance. *My cowherd friend is a giver, not a taker. When he appears to take, it is only to give something greater, like freedom. His love is so wonderful, so valuable. It is worth giving up anything to have that love. Fears, you may be true! I don't care about fears! I want love!* The looming personalities of the countless fears dissipated like fog in bright sunshine. Then, still only mentally, Avid submerged deeply into the ocean of love. He could feel the liquid warmth of love around him, through him, and in him, saturating every cell, every thought. He felt like his Supreme Friend was embracing him in an eternal hug of comradery. The presence of his main teachers—the bee-like friend who was there with him now, Keen and Sage, his primary teacher in Acumen—flooded his awareness, blessing him and encouraging him. He mentally bowed deeply to each of them, and his joy increased beyond measure.

When the stillness ceased, and Avid rose, the feeling he had had in the presence of his bee-like teacher-friend, and in the Supreme Friend the cowherd, stayed with him. If it were possible, that feeling expanded more and more by the moment, without fading. Avid walked back to his three companions as they finished eating, and then they all continued to walk. *And I thought I had seen every possible forest! How wrong, oh how very wrong, I was! How very, very wrong!* This forest which before had looked like small twisted trees of thorns, growing in sand, now looked like landscaped gardens tended and enjoyed by a highly cultured person with exquisite taste in beauty and design. There were groves with fountains, flowering and fruiting trees, flowering bushes, and pathways made of glittering stones. *The full name of this place is "Garden of Sacred Fragrance," from what the teacher told me in Acumen. A fitting name.* "It's beautiful here," Avid said, overcome with the fragrance of jasmine and ylang-ylang.

"Well, I suppose so," the group leader said distractedly. "The place is really run-down. No one takes care of it. Just thorns. There's a place nearby I like to take people to. It's pretty special."

Avid felt a soft breeze and heard the songs of a thousand different bird species. *Am I the only one experiencing all this?* The path had tall and wide trees on either side, shading the path like a tent. After a little while, the leader brought them to a small pond next to a structure.

"Here is a special pond. It's said that anyone who bathes here will regain his or her original, spiritual form," the guide said. "The trees here are in rather unusual shapes. People say they are dancing."

The other two people with Avid laughed and prepared to dip into the pond. All of them had brought other clothes for going into the water, and now changed into those clothes. After changing his clothes, Avid looked at the trees. They were, indeed, dancing! They moved slowly, yet very gracefully. Their leafy hair had flower decorations, and he gradually became aware that they were also singing. Songs of water, light, and love floated through the air—there were a thousand tree voices each singing their own song, distinct from each other yet harmonizing. The tree voices blended with birdsongs and the songs of forest creatures. Singing coming from the pond joined in as the voice of a goddess. Avid moved toward the pond, feeling as if he were dancing or possibly floating. A song flowed from him of its own accord. He entered the water until he couldn't touch the bottom, and then dived into the jade-colored depths.

There, under the water, was his dear friend, the Supreme Soul, the Supreme Self, the cowherd. He was the oldest yet youthful, beginningless and the beginning. And, as he looked at his own form, he saw it was no longer that of Avid, but of a spiritual being. His spiritual form was more real and substantial than any form of his experience. But, the greatest difference was that the spiritual form was he, himself, not a physical covering over himself nor a material machine. He felt that this spiritual form had always been there, and would always be there. It was the form of his love and his friendship. Under the water, time ceased, though Avid's three companions thought he had dipped in and out in only a moment. But Avid's experience while apparently under the water was different. In his original, spiritual form he went with the cowherd to the pastures to take care of the cows, calves, and bulls. Along with multitudes of other cowherding young boys, they danced, sang, and played games. They ate picnic lunches. Days and years went by in an endless round of games and sport. There was no time and yet there was sequence of perfect events, one after another. The world and the physical identity of Avid was forgotten beyond memory, as if it never existed, or as if it were a dream. Then, he became aware of a question, a choice. Avid chose and, suddenly, emerged out of the water to serve with love in this world. He walked to the shore. He looked to the others like the same Avid. But he now felt as if he was simultaneously in two worlds. Mostly, his awareness was on his awakened true self and his activities in the spiritual realm. To some small extent, he had awareness of the world and his conventional identity. That conventional identity was now like a cover identity, or an assumed character of an actor in a drama.

In Two Worlds

Avid spent the remainder of the six weeks living with Ucitel and the students from Acumen. But most of the day, every day, he went on his own and got to know some of the residents and, most of all, himself. He found that it was fairly easy for him to recognize another person who was awakened to his or her real spiritual identity. Such people would talk about the cowherd, the friend of all, in very intimate and personal ways. Each of those people had a unique relationship with the cowherd, a relationship that, they explained, became clearer and deeper over time.

The ideas and philosophy Avid had spoken and thought countless times to himself and others now became a living reality beyond words. *The one who is both within and without, near and far, self-illuminating and filled with love. Oh, I feel him within me, the Soul of the Soul, the essence of my very self, the essence of everything. He has always been here, in union with me. Yet, and yet, he is separate also, my friend, my beloved friend. He is... He is... Filled with love, oh, he is love itself! And I am in love!* Avid felt that all his senses were eyes seeing the beauty of his cowherd friend, and then all his senses were noses smelling his friend's fragrance, as Sage had described. Sometimes Avid would see his other friend, the celestial bee — *Oh, how could I ever have thought he was actually a bee!* — but he now could see his guide's real form. And, oh! He and his guide were eternal friends with each other and with the Supreme Friend.

The stories Avid had read many times and even memorized as if he were studying for a test now took place in his heart. He was a participant. Every word of the prayers and mantras and songs now took on life and meaning in thousands of ways which he marveled at and tried to explain. Oh, but when he tried to explain his current understanding to others who had not crossed over the veil, they would inevitably hear something distorted by their minds, and not exactly what he intended to communicate.

What was perhaps the strangest thing about this new way of living was that, externally, few people could tell he had changed. True, he was more emotionally expressive, but his personality in the world, along with its quirks and peculiarities, more or less remained. Other people might remark on how his eyes particularly shined, or how much more he laughed, or how kind he was. But only a few confidants could guess that his internal reality was fundamentally changed.

The inner landscape of the Sacred Garden was so radically different than his previous impressions that Avid marveled at the change. He no longer saw an ancient and run-down dirty place. He remained distantly aware of that impression, but it was not his personal experience anymore, as if he could see both a façade and the reality behind it at the same time. The experience was something like working on a stage for a drama, but far beyond that. The cowherd boy and his friends were there in the Sacred Garden as if not in this world at all, and not mundane. Avid felt like he had entered a portal into a secret and mysterious realm which was right in front of people, yet unseen. Sometimes he wanted to grab a passer-by and say, "Can't you see it and smell it?" But he refrained and merely laughed internally.

When the time came to journey from the Sacred Garden back to Acumen, Avid felt that his body followed the group, but his consciousness remained in the spiritual realm. It was as if he carried the essence of the Sacred Garden within himself always. What even he himself did not understand was that he had become a moving sacred place — a portal for others to experience the eternal realm just by his presence. The walking samadhi he had felt when in Dutiful for the second time was of the mind, but now his inner state was far beyond any concept of mind.

So, in that state, which increased dynamically in its own way, unfolding to Avid's wonder and amazement, he passed through many towns and cities. The traveling group took a different route to Acumen, and so he didn't go through his parents' home city. But he was regularly sending messages back and forth, though there was no way to explain his spiritual transition to them, so he didn't mention it even obliquely. His mother wrote her usual questions yet again, and he pretended he didn't see them, responding to anything else in her messages. But, in his communication with Keen and Sage, he was very explicit and described things in detail. They replied:

Keen: I like being a father and can't wait to hear all your stories. I am not as blessed as you or my wife, though one day while I meditated, I had glimpses of my eternal spiritual form and nature, which surprised me. That day I suddenly remembered the fortune teller. I feel like I have touched the treasure, at least enough to know it's real.

Sage: Avid, you are so fortunate! Keen says I'm fortunate, also. What's really strange is that I feel I have just begun my spiritual life, or as if, really, I'm not even at the beginning. We can talk more when you arrive, when the baby is sleeping and we get a chance. Oh, and I never saw that old woman I wrote you about last time leave the studio nor did I ever see her again. I looked and asked, but no one knew of anyone matching that description.

Acumen, Again

Twenty years passed since his first visit to the Garden of Sacred Fragrance. Avid had become a famous teacher in Acumen and taken strict vows of asceticism. People traveled from faraway places to study under him, and he was respected beyond the group of his particular teacher and school. In fact, not only did the various Devotional Connection school leaders come to him for general advice and personal guidance, but many teachers and students from the other connection schools sought him out—some privately if they felt that the others in their school and path were too sectarian-minded. Avid traveled every two years to the Sacred Garden, and on the way stopped by his parental home until both his parents had passed from this world. Sometimes he visited his brother and sisters, but more often they came to Acumen with their families to see him, except for Mohah who never communicated with him at all.

Keen and Sage had five children—two sons and three daughters. They spent most of their time teaching spirituality through art, rather than directly, and not in connection with a particular school, though they each had their teachers. Their oldest son, born while Avid took his first journey to the Sacred Garden, was now a beginning teacher in a Knowing Connection school. Their other children had taken courses in various schools in Acumen, and the two oldest had families of their own.

One day, their 12-year-old son Laksyah stopped by Avid's study room and asked if they could talk. Avid walked with Laksyah through one of the gardens outside his study area, and to the edge of town, going somewhat into one of the forests. They sat on rocks near a small stream where bees hovered around flowering trees. Avid was aware that his celestial friend was present though unannounced, and he internally smiled.

"I love the forest, Laksyah," Avid started. "Although I often teach in buildings, I come here whenever I can. When I was growing up, the forest meant the forest of illusion and suffering, but now the forest for me means a garden of sacred fragrance where I find my dearest friends. What would you like to talk about?"

Laksyah took some minutes to watch and listen to the stream, especially the places where the filtered sunlight danced on the water as it swirled over and around rocks. He picked up some fallen flower petals and played with them. "You've been my parents' friend for a long time, and I've sat in your classes. I've been taking classes and doing the practices for the last year in this Devotion Connection school and the search for truth is part of my family and this city." Laksyah looked at Avid, and then to the petals in his hands. Those petals were now bruised and brown, so he dropped them. He then smelled his fingers. The scent was sweet yet spicy, entering deeply into his lungs.

Avid became absorbed in the eternal play of the cowherd in his heart. He closed his eyes and divinely inspired contemplation flooded his awareness, leaving only the smallest sliver of his identity as Avid in a forest talking to Laksyah.

Laksyah wondered if "Uncle Avid," as he affectionately called him, had fallen asleep. He thought to refrain from disturbing him, and let the minutes pass like the birds and insects flying past, or the ants running through the forest litter. After a while, his reason for wanting to speak to Avid was too great, and he would risk awakening him. "Uncle Avid—"

"Yes? Oh, was I distracted?" Avid patted Laksyah on the shoulder. "I don't think you finished what you wanted to say."

"So, yes, what I already said is true, but... but... I want to go beyond officially being in a school and getting just glimpses of truth. I want to go beyond the veil. I suspect that you and my mother crossed beyond illusion long ago, and recently my father has changed in ways I can't explain. I am tired of rituals being rituals, and beliefs being beliefs. I want the real thing. I hope to find 'the essence of life, the nectar of happiness; what is both within and without, near and far; what is self-illuminating and filled with love.'"

Avid leaned back on the short, flat rock, resting his hands on the forest floor slightly behind him, and smiled. "Then, let us begin."

Notes on the Metaphors

To delve more deeply into the original allegorical stories and metaphors on which this book is based, one is encouraged to read the following works:

Srimad-Bhagavatam (1972) (A.C. Bhaktivedanta Swami Prabhupada, Trans.). Los Angeles, California: Bhaktivedanta Book Trust. (Original work published *ca.* 3000 B.C.) [The story of the merchants is found in the fifth canto, chapters 13 and 14.]

Sri Manah-siksa by Raghunatha dasa Gosvami (Hari Parshad Dasa, Trans.) (Original work published *ca.* 1560) with the commentary of Bhaktivinoda Thakura. Hillsborough, NC, USA: Padma, Inc.

Caitanya-caritamrita by Krishnadasa Kaviraja (1974) (A.C. Bhaktivedanta Swami Prabhupada, Trans.). Los Angeles, California: Bhaktivedanta Book Trust. (Original work published *ca.* 1590.) [The story of the fortune teller is in the Madhya section, chapter 20; the wild elephant and the two witches are in the Madhya section, chapter 19.]

The meanings of the many metaphorical settings and characters in this story are specifically defined in the above works in the following ways:

* *A group of travelers to a foreign land looking for cheap goods to sell at a profit* is a metaphor for embodied souls who have forgotten their spiritual identity and are in the material world where they hope to get enjoyment but are repeatedly frustrated.
* *Honeybees seeking the nectar of flowers* is a metaphor for saints and spiritual guides.
* *Tigers and jackals* is a metaphor for friends and family members who steal wealth.

- *Gadflies and mosquitoes* is a metaphor for envious and critical people.
- *Locusts, birds of prey and rats* is a metaphor for persons and circumstances which take away hard-earned wealth.
- *Mirage of castle in the sky* is a metaphor for dreams for a life of luxury and ease which never happen despite hard work.
- *Phosphorescent light in a marsh, appearing like it's fire or gold,* is a metaphor for running after wealth for happiness.
- *Dust storm* is a metaphor for uncontrolled sexual desire.
- *Owls and crickets* is a metaphor for one's unseen enemies who criticize us behind our back.
- *Snakes* is a metaphor for enemies who actively harm us.
- *Shallow rivers with sharp rocks* is a metaphor for teachers of materialistic religions.
- *Cannibalistic demons* is a metaphor for government officials who tax heavily.
- *Being attacked by bees when seeking honey* is a metaphor for illicit sexual relationships.
- *A great mountain to climb, with one's feet pricked by thorns and pebbles* is a metaphor for expensive and complex social ceremonies.
- *Python* is a metaphor for sleep.
- *Lion* is a metaphor for death.
- *Two witches* is a metaphor for taking up religion with the goal of prosperity or salvation instead of love.
- *Treasure* as spoken of by the fortune teller is a metaphor for the essence of life.
- *Snake* in the northern section is a metaphor for the desire to lose one's identity in cosmic energy.
- *Nature spirits (Yakshas)* in the western section is a metaphor for the bewilderment of trying to find truth only with the mind and intellect.
- *Elephant in musth* in the eastern section is a metaphor for the destruction of our love when we have malice towards seekers of the essence of life.

- *Hornets* in the southern section is a metaphor for rigid hierarchies and conflicts based on class and gender which only cause pain.
- *A prostitute* is a metaphor for gossip and critical talk which steals our spiritual wealth in return for false pleasure.
- *A tigress* is a metaphor for talks of liberation and disgust with life, which devours our true loving self.
- *Twisted people who put ropes around people's necks and drag them around* is a metaphor for lust, envy, anger, greed and so forth which pull otherwise spiritual people into acts of hypocrisy.
- *A bath in burning donkey urine* is a metaphor for hidden self-hypocrisy, where one's speech and actions are in line with the spiritual, but one's motives and thoughts are selfish.
- *A bath in the ocean of love* is a metaphor for the courage to seek complete truth through revelation from the Supreme.
- *A dead dog as food* is a metaphor for the honor and prestige one receives due to spiritual practices.
- *The dancing woman who eats the dead dog* is a metaphor for the desire to be honored for one's spirituality and *her lover* is a metaphor for deceit.

Cast of Characters

The meaning of each character's name indicates that character's inclination, but not the sum total of his or her persona. These names are taken from many different languages. Knowing what the names mean can add to one's appreciation of the story but is not necessary for understanding the allegories.

* **Duma** (pride) is the mother of Avid and wife of Tavis. Her other children are Mohah, Bron, Sarala, and Pena.
* **Tavis** (ordinary person) is the father of Avid and husband of Duma. His other children are Mohah, Bron, Sarala, and Pena.
* **Mohah** (illusion) is the oldest brother of Avid and the oldest child and son of Duma and Tavis. He is 19 years old in the forest section and 24 at the start of the city section.
* **Bron** (regret) is the older brother of Avid and the second child of Duma and Tavis. He is 18 years old in the forest section and 23 at the start of the city section.
* **Sarala** (simple) is the oldest sister of Avid and the third child and oldest daughter of Duma and Tavis. She is 16 years old in the forest section and 21 at the start of the city section.
* **Pena** (dissatisfaction) is the older sister of Avid and the fourth child and youngest daughter of Duma and Tavis. She is 15 years old in the forest section and 20 at the start of the city section.
* **Avid** (eager and enthusiastic, the *a* pronounced as in *apple*) is the fifth child and youngest son of Duma and Tavis. He is 11 years old (just shy of his 12th birthday) in the forest section and is 17 at the start of the city section.
* **Grandma** is Tavis's mother and Duma's mother-in-law.
* **Keen** (penetrating understanding and eagerness) is Avid's close friend of the same age.

- **Sage** (wise person) is Keen's love interest, and eventually wife, and is the same age as Keen and Avid.
- **Vitoyah** or **Vyudaka** (shallow river) is a magician in the form of a religious teacher.
- **Vahtya** (dust storm, tornado, whirlwind) is Bron's love interest.
- **Lumpatah** (playboy, debauchee) is a resident of the city and the husband of Dukha.
- **Dukha** (sorrow) is a resident of the city and the wife of Lumpatah.
- **Ucitel** (teacher) is a teacher of Devotion Connection who takes a group to the Garden of Sacred Fragrance.
- **Lajja** (shame) is a teacher of Devotion Connection in Dissemble.
- **Laksyah** (one who understands clearly) is the youngest child and son of Keen and Sage.

Acknowledgments

As this book is based on metaphors from Jada Bharata, Caitanya Mahaprabhu, and Raghunatha Das Goswami, my thanks are first of all to them. A.C. Bhaktivedanta Swami Prabhupada translated the teachings of the first two, from Sanskrit and Bengali respectively, into English, and introduced me to the ancient tradition of which they are a part. He also kindly accepted me as his student in my own quest to find the essence of life. Hari Parshad Dasa translated Das Goswami's Sri Manah-siksa (Splendid Instructions to the Mind). It was our work on the publication of that book that most inspired this one.

Phalguni Radhika Devi-dasi and Padma-gopi Walsh are the artists, each of whom produced illustrations which bring this book to life. Will Workman took the book through many edits. The final form of this book is due in large part to his encouraging and bluntly honest suggestions for improvements. I am deeply grateful for his help and insight. Kosa Ely's comment after reading what I thought was a final manuscript substantially enhanced the work, especially for part three. Jayadvaita Swami gave helpful feedback on the book and particularly improved part one.

Michael Best did a final proofreading and edit, as well as design and layout, and prepared the book for e-reader format. Several people agreed to read the manuscript and gave helpful feedback, including Philip Jones and Tessa from Mandala Publishing, Gopavrindapal, David Lloyd, Steve Magasis, Anneke Oostindie, Denise Evans, and Rebecca Gaab. My thanks are to all of them, and to everyone who gave me facility for writing while on my own many journeys.

Finally, I wish to thank those who created the "goals" feature of Google Calendar, which automatically scheduled my writing time and got me to be productive in circumstances where I thought working on a book was impossible.

About the Author

Dr. Urmila Edith Best was born and raised in New York City as the daughter of the CEO of the Manischewitz food business. She travels worldwide teaching techniques of bhakti-yoga and mantra meditation which she has practiced since 1973. She has authored *Vaikuntha Children*, a guidebook for devotional education; *The Great Mantra for Mystic Meditation*; dozens of articles; and *Dr. Best Learn to Read*, an 83-book complete literacy program with technology enabling the story books to speak in 25 languages at the touch of a special "pen." She has also produced *Sri Manah-siksa: Splendid Instructions to the Mind*. She earned her Master of School Administration and Doctor of Education degrees from the University of North Carolina at Chapel Hill, and has been a professor of Sociology and Education at Bhaktivedanta College in Belgium. Urmila and her husband entered an ascetic order (vanaprastha) in 1996. When she isn't traveling, she's writing at her home in Govardhana, India, or visiting her two sons and daughter, their lovely spouses, eight grandsons, six granddaughters, grandson-in-law, and great-grandson.

Made in the USA
Columbia, SC
15 July 2018